Ahmadou Kourouma

Les Soleils des Indépendances

Patricia O'Flaherty

Coordinator of International Education (Europe)
Ollscoil Luimnigh / University of Limerick

patricia.oflaherty@ul.ie

UNIVERSITY OF GLASGOW
FRENCH AND GERMAN PUBLICATIONS
2007

University of Glasgow French and German Publications

Modern Languages Building, 16 University Gardens,
Glasgow G12 8QL, Scotland.

In memory of Steve Irwin (1962-2006)

First published 2007.

© Copyright UNIVERSITY of GLASGOW FRENCH & GERMAN PUBLICATIONS.

All rights reserved. No part of this publication may be reproduced, stored in a retrieval system, or transmitted, in any form or by any means, electronic, mechanical, recording or otherwise, without the prior permission of the publisher.

Printed by Universities' Design and Print, Glasgow G4 0LT.

ISBN 0 85261 813 1

Contents

Introduction	1
Chapter One: Kourouma and his *œuvre*	3
Chapter Two: Context	13
History and ethnic composition	13
Independence	17
Politics	19
Chapter Three: Systems of belief	25
Islam and the Qur'an	25
Animism	28
Lineage	31
Faith-based daily life	34
a) The Muslim woman	34
b) The Muslim man	38
Chapter Four: Language	43
Verbal incongruities	44
Neologisms	47
The style of excess	49
Proverbs and precepts	51
Gross and scatological expressions	54
Chapter Five: Writing West Africa	57
Location	57
The physical and allegorical environment	63
Narration	68
a) Storytelling	69
b) Spin doctoring	75
Conclusion	82
Glossary	87
Select bibliography	91

Preface

The reference edition of *Les Soleils des Indépendances* for this Guide is the Seuil paperback, collection 'Points' P766. Page citations are given in **bold** typeface between brackets, e.g. **(24)**. The most likely English version to be available is *The Suns of Independence*, tr. Adrian Adams (New York: Holmes & Meier Publishers, 2000), ISBN 0 841 907 471.

Editions of other works consulted, and abbreviated reference titles:
Monnè, outrages et défis [*Monné*], Seuil, 'Points' P556.
En attendant le vote des bêtes sauvages [*En attendant*], Seuil, 'Points' P762.
Allah n'est pas obligé [*Allah*], Seuil, 2000.
Quand on refuse on dit non [*Quand on refuse*], Seuil, 'Points' P1377.

A valuable recent perspective on religious and ethnic tensions along the parallel now dividing the country is provided by Tony D'Souza's *Whiteman* (London: Portobello, 2006), the lightly fictionalised memoir of a volunteer's life in the Worodougou until his evacuation in 2002.

Critics' publication details may be found in the Bibliography. Single citations and works from the literary canon are referenced on the page.

Charles Forsdick, a tower of strength, is warmly thanked for his help.

Les timbres des Indépendances

Philately will get you nowhere, but collections have been ransacked for the facing miscellany, reflecting the 'Bliss was it in that dawn to be alive' mood of some African states at the time of 'les Indépendances'. The stern, warlike countenance of General Léon Faidherbe, mythical «Fadarba» of Senegal in the 1860s (see *Monné*, p. 18), when compared to the bland, media-savvy expression of Valéry Giscard d'Estaing, paying a state visit to Guinea's Sékou Touré in 1978, bears eloquent testimony to the 'Afrique en marche' evolution that has taken place

Two later Côte d'Ivoire stamps depict the divisive symbol of the largest basilica in the world, copying St Peter's in Rome, consecrated by Pope John Paul II. Conflation of Coleridge ('In Xanadu did Kubla Khan / A stately pleasure-dome decree') with Shelley ('Nothing beside remains') is as irresistible as, in the light of recent events, it is impudent.

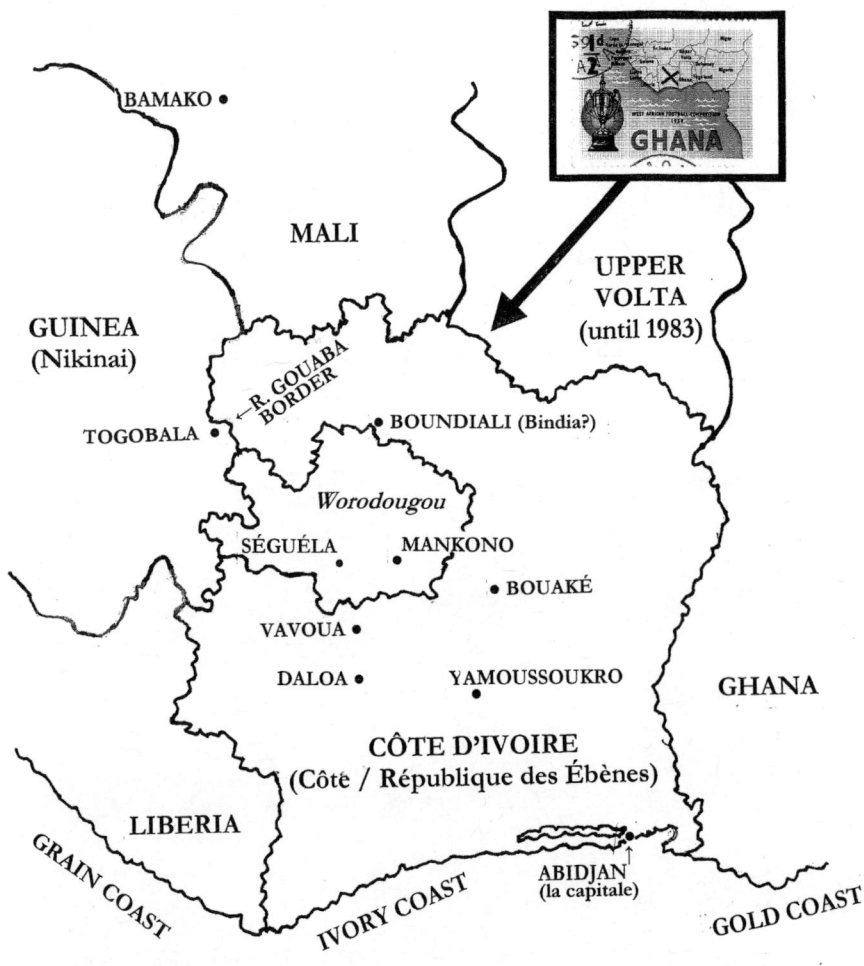

The above map details locations in both fact (upper-case) and fiction (lower-case); Worodougou (italicised) belongs to each category. There are only 2 feasible routes for Fama's journey home; he appears to overnight at Kourouma's birthplace of Boundiali (Bindia?), soon after which 'Déja la camionnette roulait sur les terres de la province de Horodougou' (**99**), which in his eyes stretches far to the west, into Guinea, and particularly the north, into Mali. If the 2,000-plus kilometres travelled by Koné Ibrahima's shade (**9**) were to be taken literally (a big if, admittedly), then unfettered by border controls and able to travel rectilinearly in the blink of an eye, it might have reached into the cradle of Malinké civilisation as far as Bamako.

Introduction

Ahmadou Kourouma's *Les Soleils des Indépendances* was published in the same watershed year for metropolitan France (1968) as Yambo Ouologuem's *Le Devoir de violence* (Prix Renaudot). Following in the footsteps of Ferdinand Oyono, both present a jaundiced picture of African society, satirising the exploitation of the colonists and the dire consequences of their postcolonial legacy (bad governance; greed; cronyism; favouritism and / or persecution of ethnic groups and religions), as well as portraying the social and religious practices of traditional African society in a realistic, unsentimentalised light. Kourouma's sour yet impish chronicle updates so boldly as to relate broadly recognisable events at but two years' remove. His account of the sterile harmattan season of discontent (**32**) of a traumatised victim of female genital cutting and her infertile parasite of a husband, himself much older and colder (**162**), paints, like J.M. Coetzee's novel *Disgrace* (Booker Prize, 1999) a dark picture of a tragic continent.

In Doumbouya family lore, a voice proclaims from on high that a forebear's treachery will lead to the extinction of the line:

> Il se fera un jour où le soleil ne se couchera pas, où des fils d'esclaves, des bâtards lieront toutes les provinces avec des fils, des bandes et du vent, et commanderont, où tout sera pleutre, éhonté […]. (**99**)

This enigmatic prediction was interpreted, with self-serving 'spin', to mean Judgment Day; but wholesale appropriation of communications ('des fils'), road-building ('des bandes') and media ('le vent') resources by the politically unscrupulous, in a country where the sun need never set '(les lampes électriques éclairant toute la nuit dans la capitale'--**100**), means that the day of wrath has arrived earlier than expected, by the year 1960. Fama's life may be considered to be the clearest of metaphors of the unpalatable consequences of this:

> Une vie qui se mourait, se consumait dans la pauvreté, la stérilité, l'Indépendance et le parti unique! Cette vie-là n'était-elle pas un soleil éteint et assombri dans le haut de sa course? (**31**)

To date, critics have viewed Ahmadou Kourouma as above all an innovative writer, in terms of his use of language. There has been a great deal of critical material published in French on the work of Kourouma, particularly on this, his first novel. Most studies concentrate on his innovative use of language, with several treating the oral nature of the style. Other topics of research are the novel's social and political content, the influence of history, and narrative technique. Six books have been published in French on Kourouma, including a general study of his fiction, an analysis of the Africanised French of Kourouma's writings, and a study of myth in *Les Soleils des Iindépendances*. If not many articles, and no books to date, have been written in English on Kourouma, it suggests that this major West African author deserves more exposure in the anglophone world.

Although the novel is among the first in a new wave of African writing, *Les Soleils des Indépendances* nonetheless draws on the writings of the previous generation of African writers. In respect of structure, Kourouma is the heir of the Senegalese writer Cheikh Hamidou Kane. Like Kane's *L'Aventure ambiguë*, his work has a classical three-part structure, the first and last parts having mainly to do with the capital city of a fictitious but clearly recognisable republic, and the middle part being situated in Fama's home village, Togobala (**98**), for long not mentioned by name because of its identity being subservient to the mythical dynastic prestige of the homeland of Worodougou ('Horodougou' is sometimes, as here, the French transliteration). At the end of the novel, Fama's journey will take him back, with an irrational but comprehensible homing instinct, to his birthplace. In *L'Aventure ambiguë*, Samba Diallo journeys from his home village to the capital, then to Paris and, finally, in the third part of the novel, returns to his home, where, like Fama, he will die (see Mortimer, pp. 108; 109-10; 116-7). This notion of a long and arduous journey—'Un voyage de cette espèce cassait l'échine d'un homme de l'âge de Fama' (**92**)—, constituting a quest, is common to both novels.

Kourouma is a supremely talented writer, and the reader will not be long in appreciating in him a superior degree of narrative competence, and a relaxed mastery of the registers of humour and pathos alike.

Chapter One

Kourouma and his *œuvre*

Ahmadou Kourouma was the eldest son of a distinguished Malinké family of royal lineage in former times; the deferential name of Moriba, conferred on Fama's ancestor Souleymane Doumbouya (**97**), is his late father's forename. Born in Boundiali (Côte d'Ivoire) on 24 November 1927, he was brought up as a Muslim by his uncle Niankoro, a combination of male nurse, hunter and witch doctor, and initially pursued his studies in Mali. The formative influence of both of these men is recognised in the dedication to his third novel:

> À toi, regretté tonton **Niankoro Fondio**,
> saluts et respects!
> À toi, regretté papa **Moriba Kourouma**,
> saluts et respects!
> À vous,
> deux émérites maîtres chasseurs à jamais disparus!
> Votre neveu et fils dédie ces veillées
> et sollicite encore, encore,
> votre protection, vos bénédictions.
>
> (*En attendant*, p. 7)

Between 1950 and 1954, when his country was still under French colonial rule, after losing his *tirailleur*'s stripes for refusing to help put down popular unrest there he was sent to be trained in France, and thence to Indochina, where he participated in military campaigns. After this, he studied mathematics in Lyon and qualified as an actuary in 1959. Kourouma returned to a job in a bank in his native Côte d'Ivoire after independence, in 1961, but was critical of the government of Félix Houphouët-Boigny (1905-1993) and was hit with redundancy and a spell of imprisonment (though shorter than Fama's). He spent many years working in various African countries, first Algeria (1965-1969), then Côte d'Ivoire again (1970-1972), until his play *Tougnatigui*, performed in Abidjan, caused further trouble, Cameroon (1974-1983) and Togo (1983-1993), before he returned to live in Côte d'Ivoire, after which he moved to France. He died in Lyon during an operation on a benign tumour (11 December 2003).[1]

The founding fathers of the *négritude* movement, Aimé Césaire and Léopold Senghor, and the first generation of African writers, including Ferdinand Oyono, Sembene Ousmane, Cheikh Hamidou Kane and Camara Laye, condemned the evils of colonialism and praised the values of pre-colonial Africa, laying the foundations for pride in African identity and looking forward to the promised land of post-independence African countries. The new generation of poets, playwrights and novelists, including Henri Lopes, Sony Labou Tansi, Williams Sassine, Tierno Monénembo, Boris Diop, Emmanuel Dongala, Alain Mabanckou and Abdhourahman A. Waberi, as well as Kourouma, are also, of course, critical of the colonial period, but they focus as well on the terrible ills of post-independence Africa, where so many constituents of elected members of government are unemployed, scraping an existence from the soil or from the black economy that somehow functions in cities across Africa from Mombasa to Dakar and from Algiers to Cape Town.

Kourouma has published five novels, one play and several stories for children. His first novel, *Les Soleils des Indépendances*, first published in Canada in 1968 and by Éditions du Seuil in France in 1970, won three literary prizes (Prix de la Tour-Landry de l'Académie Française; Prix de la Francité [Montréal]; Prix de l'Académie royale de Belgique). The rest of Kourouma's literary production was written after his retirement from a professional career as an actuary. His second novel, which appeared in 1990, has the challenging and intriguing title of *Monnè, outrages et défis*, one which emphasises Kourouma's desire to introduce the reader to specifically African concepts; it gained the accolades of the Prix des Nouveaux Droits de l'Homme, the Prix CIRTEF and the Grand Prix de l'Afrique noire. The polysemy of the notion of 'monné', or *monnew* in the Malinké language, does not translate conveniently into French or

---

[1] Some of this detail is extracted from Patrick Corcoran's useful obituary notice (see bibliography).

English. The authorial epigraph to the novel (p. 9) explains that a whole series of words such as 'outrage, défis, mépris, injures, humiliations, colère rageuse' serve to convey the meaning of *monnè*; later, another synonym, 'amertume' (p. 153), is ventured. The three evocative words of the title *Monnè, outrages et défis* refer to colonialism, which constitutes the subject of the novel. In fact, the novel is situated at the very beginning of the colonial era and centres on the figure of the king of Soba, Djigui Keita, who disobeys Samory Touré, emperor of the Manding territory, a real-life historical figure who successfully combated the colonial powers until an alliance between the French and the English prevented him from sourcing guns. Samory issued an edict commanding his subjects to destroy their villages rather than submit to the colonial invasion.[2]

The theme of the novel is Djigui's life and his collaboration with the enemy, the colonists. Although the novel's chronology coincides with that of Djigui's reign under the French, there are references to more ancient times and customs. The novel is, therefore, part history, part fiction and, on another level still, constitutes a satirical commentary on present-day regimes in Africa, where ordinary people compromise their aspirations, and those of their ancestors who fought against colonialism, by accepting the more and more ludicrously destructive, power-hungry policies of political leaders. Djigui, also referred to as 'le Centenaire', is a complex character, shifting with the times as he reluctantly works with the French, trying to maintain his integrity and the traditions of his people, gradually losing his once hegemonic grip, and finally being betrayed by his son Béma. The worst excesses of the colonial era, specifically forced labour, a twentieth-century form of slavery, are exposed in all their horror. Well-known actual events, such as Stanley's expedition (*En attendant*, pp. 228-9) and the true agendas behind events such as the driving of the railway deep into Côte d'Ivoire (*Monnè*, p. 73 *et passim*; the 'suprême monnè' [p. 278] is when it is decreed that it will not, after all, pass through Soba) form part of the narrative. French

---

[2] Unsurprisingly, the Samorian wars of the 1890s against a French invading force led by Faidherbe are referred to in *Soleils* as a heroic age of non-'bastardised' chivalry (**18; 112**); see also *Allah*, p. 97.

politics intrude, in the persons of Pétain and de Gaulle, as European history is portrayed from an African point of view. Other characters' stories are woven into this tapestry: that of the interpreter Soumaré, that of Moussokoro, Djigui's favourite wife, that of Djéliba the griot. The latter is the principal narrator, but the narration shifts constantly (for instance, Djigui sometimes relates events in the first person). The narrative point of view adopted is vitally important, as the wide range of perspectives implies that there are any numbers of truths and any number of versions of history, depending on one's cultural standpoint (see **98**: 'Il existe une autre version'). As throughout Kourouma's writing, the act of storytelling is commented on in terms of traditional African custom, for example, in the following observation, 'Quand un homme part définitivement, le premier devoir des survivants est de parler de lui.' (*Monnè*, p. 217), which is repeated by the child soldier, Birahima, narrator of Kourouma's last two novels, *Allah n'est pas obligé* (see pp. 94; 100) and *Quand on refuse on dit non* (recalling genocide at Yopougon and Monoko Zohi).

Kourouma's third novel, *En attendant le vote des bêtes sauvages* (1998), is also a prizewinning work (Prix Tropiques; Grand Prix de la Société des Gens de Lettres; Prix du Livre Inter). It is his most ambitious and most important work in terms of form and content, portraying the vast panorama of African politics over the last thirty years. The epic genre is even more evident in this novel than it was in *Monnè, outrages et défis*, in that the six-part structure is that of the *donsomana*, the purificatory narrative or praise song, pronounced as a funeral oration for the dead. The formal praise song, related by Bingo, griot poet to the dictator Koyaga, and the latter's jester Tiécoura, must tell the truth, in order to be effective as a means of facilitating the passage of the soul into the afterlife, and relate all the tyrant's qualities and flaws. This genre provides the author with the opportunity to reveal the full extent of cruel, ruthless dictatorship in modern Africa and to comment indirectly on the role of the West in installing and maintaining these destructive genocidal regimes. *En attendant le vote des bêtes sauvages* tells the story of Koyaga, the prototypical African dictator, who rules over the 'République du Golfe'. His life and rule are clearly based on those of Gnassingbé

Eyadema (1935-2005), who ruled Togo for thirty-eight years until his death. Kourouma presents history as myth, coloured by the supernatural and the superhuman. Koyaga is a master hunter and, whereas the 'confrérie des griots' dominated the narrative form in *Monnè, outrages et défis*, the brotherhood of the hunters prevails in *En attendant le vote des bêtes sauvages*. Kourouma, in accordance with the epic mode, returns to the source by first relating the story of Koyaga's father, Tchao. Turning to prehistory, the narration mocks European ethnologists who named Tchao's people Paleonegritic or 'Paleos'. Tchao is a heroic wrestler and the first of his people to fight for the French, in World War One. On returning to his native lands he has to choose between reverting to nakedness or wearing clothes so he can display his medals. Tchao's triumphs are a victory for the white colonisers, for his people are subject to the dictates of the *Toubabs* and lose their autonomy (cf. **186**, 'Sans les Toubabs…'). The heroic warrior dies ignominiously in prison when Koyaga is seven.

Koyaga's surrogate father is a *marabout*, or Muslim holy man; his mother, a sorceress. Even as a child Koyaga is a great hunter; he too serves in the French military, in Vietnam, and becomes a hero. His political career begins much like that of Eyadema, leading a protest by veterans against the first president of Togo (Sylvanus Olympio [see stamps on p. v], portrayed in the novel as Fricassa Santos). The clash that pits Koyaga and Santos against each other is vividly presented in the guise of magic realism. The narrative moves beyond the rational as Koyaga gains power. His rule is recounted in colourful, graphic detail using a highly rhetorical format: there are assassination attempts (which he miraculously survives), socialist and other plots, foreign powers to take advantage of, monuments to build. Koyaga shows no mercy to those who oppose him. A mighty hunter of men as well as animals, he emasculates his victims and stuffs their penises and scrotums into their mouths, in the animistic belief that this will prevent their spirits taking revenge on him.

Koyaga's training as a dictator involves visiting other heads of State who are already well established. In the end, these same evil rulers pay him homage by sending spies to take note of his methods. Part of the ludic nature of the text involves, as we have seen, substituting fictional names or identities closely related to the real ones. Besides Eyadema and Santos, the astute reader recognises Guinea's Sékou Touré (see p. v) in Nkoutigi Fondio, Côte d'Ivoire's Félix Houphouët-Boigny (see p. v) in Tiékoroni, the Central African Republic's 'Emperor', Jean-Bédel Bokassa, in 'Bossouma, l'homme au totem hyène', Morocco's King Hassan II in the man of the jackal totem, Congo-Zaïre's Mobuto Sese Seko in 'l'homme au totem léopard', Patrice Lumumba, to be ousted from his premiership by Congo president Joseph Kasavubu (see p. v), in Pace Humba, Belgium's King Léopold II in Paul II, and Ethiopia's Haile Selassie in the dictator with the lion totem. The same technique is employed to refer to countries, showing that borders and names have been arbitrarily decided by colonial powers. A further result of this onomastic game is to distance the reader and allow the indirect commentary of the author to make us consider the political situation seriously. One such satirical observation is the following:

> C'étaient les mânes des ancêtres qui l'avaient nommé, lui, l'homme-léopard, le chef de l'authenticité, le Père de la nation. Il disposait de toute la nation et en usait. Les décisions d'un empereur ont besoin d'être confirmées par des élus; celles d'un chef africain pas. […] Un empereur contient ses dépenses dans un budget; un vrai chef authentique africain dispose de tout l'argent du Trésor et de la Banque centrale et personne ne compte, ne contrôle ce qu'il dépense. […] Un chef africain est nettement supérieur à un empereur, conclut l'homme au totem léopard et il vous conseilla d'appliquer, comme système de gouvernement, l'authenticité. C'était le gouvernement qui convenait aux Africains. (*En attendant*, pp. 240-1)

The novel is a scathing critique of post-independence Africa and the dictators who survived with the connivance of the neocolonialist West, anxious to save Africa from communism during the Cold War.

The employment of a plethora of words to convey a rich linguistic and cultural heritage, that of West Africa, is an important feature of Kourouma's last two novels. *Allah n'est pas obligé* (2000), falling one vote shy of the Prix Goncourt but harvesting the Prix Renaudot, the Prix Goncourt des lycéens and the Prix Amerigo Vespucci, is narrated by a young boy, Birahima. When he is orphaned and lost, he becomes a child soldier and is caught up in the 'guerre tribale' (p. 53 *et passim*) of regional conflict and the outrages perpetrated by the corrupt and evil leaders of various West African countries, especially Liberia and Sierra Leone, in the mid-1990s. The names of these 'bandits de grand chemin' (p. 53) are cited directly in this text. Amongst others are Foday Sankoh, Prince Johnson and Charles Taylor, the two first-mentioned of whom are now dead and the third to appear before an international war crimes tribunal.

The child joins the marauding, unpaid bands who carry out murder and terror against civilian populations, and has to hack his way through 'des forêts de symboles' in the sense of a dense jungle of acronyms denoting warring factions (NPFL; ULIMO; LPC; ACRM; RUF), political alliances (CFA; OUA; AOF; CDEAO; AFRIC), NGOs (French: 'ONG'), i.e. non-governmental agencies aiding children in particular (72), refugees or debt-ridden countries (HCR; FMI), and peacekeeping forces (ONU; ECOMOG). Birahima's only adult companion is Yacouba, alias Tiécoura, a 'multiplicateur de billets' (p. 39), or counterfeiter. He proposes himself as the guardian of the boy as they head into Liberia, on their way to find Birahima's faraway aunt, hoping to find family and stability. Birahima is an engaging guide, a self-educated youth who enlists the help of four dictionaries that used to belong to a Malinké interpreter as he vigorously and vividly portrays his 'chienne de vie' (p. 101). Words are translated, or given pedantic explanatory glosses *à la* Lemony Snicket, but much more repetitively for gross or blasphemous words such as *gnamakodé* (*bâtard*; *bâtardise*; *putain de ma mère*), *Walahé!* (*au nom d'Allah*), *faforo* (*sexe du père*), *gnoussou-gnoussou* (vagina) and *bangala* (penis). In this text, the overt emphasis on words, with Birahima providing several different terms for one meaning, acts as an effective rhetorical tool which comments on the diversity of West Africa and also, subtly, on the lack of knowledge of the average Westerner. Birahima is irreverent about almost everything; he seems justified in demonstrating so much 'attitude', as his only hope of survival lies in this irrepressible spirit. The overt consideration by the narrator of alternative words in various languages, dialects and registers is a device whereby the novel draws upon a whole range of references, applicable to Africa, to certain tribal groups in Africa, and to the Western reader, as well as to specific time periods, such as the days of colonialism.

Birahima refers to his account as his 'blablabla' (p. 9), thereby placing the accent of the narrative on the real, the everyday, recounting a narrative that is totally lacking in any literary pretentiousness. Kourouma draws upon a whole range of references from a diverse linguistic, social and cultural archive. The commentary of the young narrator raises the issue of class in African society, a question which is frequently forgotten in the debate on race. An important theme of *Allah n'est pas obligé* and *Quand on refuse on dit non* is Birahima's lack of education and his aspiration to recount his tale in intelligible French; he is at great pains to find 'le mot juste', even if, frequently, this is a swearword. The outcome of his struggle with language is a refreshing and inspiring text, particularly given the subject matter. In creating a young, uneducated narrator, whose nobility as a human being sustains the narrative, Kourouma seems, on one level, to be satirising the members of elite, educated society in Africa, the aid workers and the new African middle class, who are unflatteringly compared with the young hero / narrator. One such instance is Birahima's comment about those who can afford to undertake the pilgrimage to Mecca:

> Chez nous, tout le monde connaît les noms de tous les grands quelqu'uns originaires du village qui ont plein d'argent à Abidjan, Dakar, Bamako, Conakry, Paris, New York, Rome et même dans les pays lointains et froids de l'autre côté de l'Océan en Amérique et en France là-bas. Les grands quelqu'uns sont appelés aussi hadjis parce qu'ils vont tous les ans à La Mecque pour égorger là-bas dans le désert leurs moutons de la grande fête musulmane appelée fête des moutons ou el-kabeir. (p. 38)

Birahima's convoluted personal saga is recounted side by side with that of the West African warlords and the atrocities they commit. Birahima takes part in these atrocities; he relates the full horror of his exploits and, following the griot tradition, gives voice to the lives led by his companions who have died in battle. Rhetorical devices characterising the oral tradition are an integral part of the narrative method, comprising recurrent refrains, direct address to the reader or listener, the use of proverb and dictum, and frequent resort to expletives. The definitive and full title of his account is: 'Allah n'est pas obligé d'être juste dans toutes ses choses ici-bas.' In this simple phrase, the gist of which is to be found in *Les Soleils des Indépendances* (see **58** [the chapter heading 'Où a-t-on vu Allah s'apitoyer sur un malheur?']; **63**) and taken up as the title of this novel, Kourouma poses the problem of evil and the incomprehension of man at man's limitless capacity for wickedness. The tragedy of Birahima's acceptance of his way of life and his factual account of the endless, bloody violence of his world is the most shocking aspect of the text, encapsulated in the phrase: 'Allah fait ce qu'il veut'. The child-narrator remains wilfully individualistic, not completely corrupted and destroyed by his terrible experiences. His adventures finally bring him back to members of his family in Côte d'Ivoire, where he may be able to take up his life and his education. Fate is once more against him, however, as Kourouma's next novel reveals.

Quand on refuse on dit non (2003) is the novelist's last work, and remained in an unfinished state when he died; at that time he had written three parts of it, as well as a synopsis of Part Four, the first pages of this part, and a fragment of a later part of the novel, entitled 'La Rébellion du Grand Ouest'. The title is no mere pleonasm, but tellingly intertextual with respect to the *œuvre*, in that an epigraph (p. 7) cites this 'fameuse parole samorienne' of Djigui Keita (*Monnè*, p. 266), provoked by the last of an apparently unending series of exactions levied and humiliations heaped on him and his tribe by the white man; in context, it means 'the last straw'. As it stands, *Quand on refuse* tells the story of Côte d'Ivoire's descent into internecine conflict and the historical reasons for the onset of violence. Birahima has survived the civil wars in Sierra Leone and Liberia, and has returned to Côte d'Ivoire, to the town of Daloa, where he lives with his cousin Mamadou Doumbia, a doctor. Birahima is an apprentice mechanic and is even learning the Qur'an from an imam called Haïdara, whose daughter is the beautiful Fanta, the object of his love. Life is at last looking hopeful for Birahima, but the novel is set in the first years of the millennium, and civil war breaks out (19 September 2002).

After a massacre in the town of Daloa, during which the cousin is machine-gunned down along with other members of the Dioula community and their religious leaders, the imams, Birahima finds himself fleeing with his beloved Fanta. The girl, who is older than her companion, does not return his feelings, but takes him along on her journey to the northern town of Bouaké, where she will become part of her uncle's household. Fanta chooses Birahima as her travelling companion because he knows how to use a Kalachnikov and will protect her, as indeed he does. Fanta decides to educate Birahima en route, and relates the history of the Côte d'Ivoire from ancient times to the present of the novel. Kourouma uses this device to describe what is known about prehistorical times, to chronicle the events of the colonial period, the way in which Houphouët-Boigny came to power, and to unravel the background and the actual events of Côte d'Ivoire's recent, bloody history. Fanta's lessons are interrupted by the people the travellers encounter, their adventures involving escape from the fighting and from the massacres happening around them, providing clarification about the real events taking place in a country being torn apart by civil war.

Individuals suffer and die, the geographical boundaries of the countries are redefined, but in Kourouma's work there is the sense of a life force which continues in spite of everything that threatens to destroy and wipe out a people and a way of life. Each event, person, alliance, marriage or birth is part of a long story or history which must be recounted and listened to in order to appreciate the full sense of present reality. The litany of ancestors, of names and of alliances reminds the reader of the beginning of the books of the Old Testament. Kourouma values genealogy as a means of bringing to life African identity and making the reader aware of a past which existed long before the colonial era, as well as of a future which will exist long after colonial and post-independence times:

> Le conseil secret des anciens palabra, évoqua les choses anciennes: Fama resterait le chef coutumier, Babou le président officiel. Et les choses futures aussi: les soleils des Indépendances passeront comme les soleils de Samory et des Toubabs, alors que les Babou, les Doumbouya, resteront toujours à Togobala. **(136)**

Chapter Two

Context

History and ethnic composition

Côte d'Ivoire, once called the Côte des Mâles Gens (i.e. ferocious warriors), appears in encyclopaedic dictionaries until after the turn of the century as 'Côte des Dents ou d'Ivoire', referring to the major cash crop of elephant tusks now superseded by cocoa, and is conceptualised in terms of its seaboard, situated between the 'Côte des Graines ou du Poivre' (Guinea) and the 'Côte d'Or' (Ghana) in the Gulf of Guinea, rather than its hinterland. This uncertainty over designation reflects a pacification by French forces that took place at a later time (the 1890s) than 'Sénégal (colonie du)', already controlled by General Faidherbe's forces in the sixties and the subject of a developed descriptive entry in the Larousse *Grand Dictionnaire Universel* by 1875. It is a relative neglect that is explained by Kourouma in economic terms: 'La Côte d'Ivoire fut épargnée par la grande traite des esclaves à cause de l'inhospitalité de la côte et parce qu'il n'y avait pas de grands royaumes négriers ivoiriens' (*Quand on refuse*, pp. 57-58).

Côte d'Ivoire's colonial history began in 1469 with the Portuguese, who created trade depots at Assini (near the Gold Coast [now Ghana] border) and Sassandra (*ibid.*, p. 57). In 1637, Dutch missionaries landed at Assini; early missions involved but a few of these because of the forbidding coastline referred to above and prospective settlers' fear of the inhabitants. In the eighteenth century, the country was invaded from present-day Ghana by two related Akan groups: the Agnis, who occupied the south-east, and the Baoulés, who settled in the central section. In 1843-1844, Admiral Bouet-Williaumez signed treaties with the kings of the

Grand Bassam and Assini regions, placing their territories under a French protectorate. Explorers, missionaries, trading companies and soldiers gradually extended the area under French control inland from the lagoon area.

Côte d'Ivoire officially became a French colony in 1893 after victory over the Mandinkas. Captain Binger, who along with Marcel Treich-Laplène had explored the Gold Coast frontier, was named the first governor. He negotiated boundary treaties with Liberia and the United Kingdom (for the Gold Coast) and fought a military campaign against Samory Touré, a Malinké chief referred to in Kourouma's novel *Monnè, outrages et défis*. From 1904 to 1958, Côte d'Ivoire was a constituent unit of the Federation of French West Africa. It was a colony and an overseas territory under the French Third Republic. Until the period following World War Two, governmental affairs in French West Africa were administered from Paris. France's policy in West Africa was reflected mainly in its philosophy of 'association', meaning that all Africans in Côte d'Ivoire were officially French 'subjects' without rights to citizenship or representation in Africa or France.

During World War Two, France's Vichy régime remained in control until 1943, when members of General Charles de Gaulle's provisional government assumed control of all French West Africa. The Brazzaville Conference in 1944, the first Constituent Assembly of the French Fourth Republic in 1946, and France's gratitude for African loyalty during World War Two led to far-reaching governmental reforms in 1946. French citizenship was granted to all African 'subjects', the right to organise politically was recognised, and various forms of forced labour were abolished. A turning point in relations with France was reached with the 1956 Overseas Reform Act (*loi Cadre*), which transferred a number of powers from Paris to elected territorial governments in French West Africa and also removed remaining voting inequalities.

The country has more than sixty ethnic groups, usually classified into five principal divisions: Akan (east and centre, including the lagoon peoples of the south-east); Krou (south-west); Southern Mandé (west); Northern Mandé (north-west); Sénoufo / Lobi (north centre and north-east). The Baoulés, in the Akan division, probably comprise the single largest subgroup, with 15%-20% of the population. They are based in the central region around Bouaké and Yamoussoukro. The Bétés in the Krou division, the Sénoufos in the north, and the Malinkés in the north-west and the cities are the next largest groups, with 10%-15% each of the national population. In *Quand on refuse on dit non*, through the perception of the youthful narrator, 'petit Birahima', Kourouma provides some insight into the tribal rivalries which constitute one of the causes of the present conflict in Côte d'Ivoire: 'le peuplement du pays a une importance majeure dans le conflit actuel. À cause de l'ivoirité. L'ivoirité signifie l'ethnie qui a occupé l'espace ivoirien avant les autres' (p. 55). President Bédié exacerbated divisions by instigating this policy. Birahima, like Fama, is a member of the Malinké group of people, who come from the North and are Sunni Muslims, whereas the Bétés are Christian and, according to the narrator, consider themselves to be the true 'Ivoiriens' and regard the Dioulas, a smaller group, part of the Malinké people, as interlopers and rogues.

One of Kourouma's aims in writing is to redress the balance in respect of African history. Western sources usually proclaim that the early history of Côte d'Ivoire is virtually unknown, but this means that the West knows little about African history prior to the colonial period. This assumption blithely ignores the existence of history known by the inhabitants of the countries concerned, whose traditions, customs, genealogy and history have been passed on from generation to generation by word of mouth. It also ignores the fact that, whilst most European countries have been extensively investigated archaeologically, African countries have not. Human settlement has, of course existed, but has not thus far been fully documented. This is one aspect highlighted by Kourouma's work. Another of Kourouma's aims is subtly to point out that the Western version of more recent African history is entirely based on a certain political stance. *Les Soleils des Indépendances* originates in the writer's desire to bear witness to the arrest of his friends. This fact belies the Western perception that the Côte d'Ivoire was, until the 1999 coup, a model of economic and political stability. Kourouma's novel makes it quite clear that Félix Houphouët-Boigny, president of the republic and leader of the Parti Démocratique de la Côte d'Ivoire (PDCI) until his death on 7 December 1993, was far from benevolent, and that daily life for the ordinary inhabitants of the country after independence was characterised by poverty and repression. Houphouët-Boigny was one of the founders of the Rassemblement Démocratique Africain (RDA), the leading pre-independence political party in French West African territories (except Mauritania).

Houphouët-Boigny, a Baoulé, first came to political prominence in 1944 as founder of the Syndicat Agricole Africain, an organisation that won improved conditions for African farmers and formed a nucleus for the PDCI. After World War Two, he was elected by a narrow margin to the first Constituent Assembly. Representing Côte d'Ivoire in the French National Assembly from 1946 to 1959, he devoted much of his effort to interterritorial political organisation and further amelioration of labour conditions. After his thirteen-year service in the Assemblée nationale, including almost three years as a minister in the French Government, he became Côte d'Ivoire's first prime minister in April 1959, and the following year was elected its first president. This background is significant in that the first leader of the country had been a member of the French government, underlining the fact that France's ties with Côte d'Ivoire meant that much of the country's economic production was turned into profit to the benefit of French interests. Kourouma is at pains to point out that colonialism was not accepted by the peoples of Côte d'Ivoire, but that, for reasons of expediency, resistance to French occupation has been glossed over by official histories of the period:

> Houphouët [...] avait une conception curieuse de l'histoire des peuples. Pour s'entendre avec le colonisateur, il a effacé la résistance à la colonisation. Il a parlé des vainqueurs et a oublié les vaincus. Il a laissé les vaincus dans l'ombre de l'oubli. (*Quand on refuse*, p. 59)

A major theme of Kourouma's fiction is collaboration, and his condemnation of this policy is encapsulated in the intertextual promotion of the defiant but unavailing words of Djigui Keita to the status of title to this final novel (on 'the last straw', see *supra*, p. 11).

Independence

Territorial borders within French West Africa had been drawn in 1904 (*Quand on refuse*, p. 57), though unsurprisingly Fama, born in or around the following year, insists on stating his birthplace to be 'Togobala (Horodougou)' (**162**). In December 1958, Côte d'Ivoire became a semi-autonomous republic within the French community as a result of a referendum that brought community status to all members of the old Federation of French West Africa except Guinea, which had voted against association. Côte d'Ivoire became independent on 7 August 1960, the same year as Chad, Togo, Nigeria, Mali, Ghana, Senegal and Benin followed suit—hence the plural and capitalisation of 'Indépendances' in the novel?—, and permitted its community membership to lapse. It appeared from the outside as a politically stable country following its independence from France in 1960 until late 1999. Under Félix Houphouët-Boigny, president from independence until his death in December 1993, Côte d'Ivoire maintained a close political allegiance to the West. His successor, President Henri Konan Bédié, served as Côte d'Ivoire's first ambassador to the U.S. Falling world market prices for the primary cash crops of cocoa and coffee put pressure on the economy and the Bédié presidency. Government corruption and mismanagement led to steep reductions in foreign aid in 1998 and 1999, and eventually to the country's first coup on 24 December 1999. This is the official version of events.

In *Quand on refuse on dit non*, Kourouma provides an unofficial take on the background to this coup, and to the conflict which is still ongoing. As noted above, Houphouët-Boigny and his successor Bédié favoured close relations with France, and neocolonialism was endorsed by those in power. The alternative history presented in *Quand on refuse*, through the history lessons given by Fanta to Birahima on their long journey from Daloa to Bouaké, shows that the seeds of conflict were sown by Houphouët's policy of importing manpower in the form of French *coopérants* and non-nationals from neighbouring countries. The narrator claims that this created a two-tier system whereby, even when local people were employed to do the same job as foreigners, they were paid less; this situation resulted in corruption and eventual conflict. These problems were exacerbated by Bédié, of the Bété ethnicity, and his policy of 'ivoirité', an attempt to distinguish those really entitled to claim citizenship from those who were not. The narrator of *Quand on refuse on dit non* indicates that this policy led to discrimination against the Northern peoples and was the real reason for the coup which brought Gueï, an army officer from the North, to power.

The elections which followed the coup did not, however, go according to Gueï's plan. His rival, Alassane Ouattara, was sidelined from the elections in 2000 because of his foreign parentage, and Gueï promised the post of prime minister to Laurent Gbagbo, an old socialist rival who had spent fifty years of his life in prison or in exile. Gbagbo, however, turned the tables on Gueï, won the presidential elections through fraudulent means, and declared himself president, finding protection at the French Embassy and having his victory quickly recognised by France and the U.S. A massacre of the Northerners followed, referred to in the text as the 'charnier de Yopougon' (*Quand on refuse*, pp. 21-22; 122). On the night of 19-20 September 2002, while Gbagbo was out of the country, an attack was mounted by army officers from the North. Kourouma states in the novel that there were, in fact, two attempted coups, one real and one manufactured by Gbagbo in order to rid himself of his enemies. Whether this is true or not, the period from 1999 to the present in the Côte d'Ivoire has been marked by terrible violence. Thousands have been killed. Athough the fighting has stopped, Ivory Coast is tense and divided. French and U.N. peacekeepers patrol the buffer zone, along the latitude of the Haut-Sassandra / Worodougou border, north of Vavoua (see map, p. vi), which separates the North, held by the rebel *Forces Nouvelles*, from the government-controlled South. Peace talks brokered by other African nations and France have, so far, failed to reunite the country. Under a 2003 peace deal the government is to disband loyalist militias and pass political reforms. In return, the *Forces Nouvelles* are to lay down their weapons. But disarmament has yet to begin.

In late September 2006, prime minister Charles Konan Banny announced his government's resignation, after hundreds of people protested against the dumping of toxic waste in Abidjan by a tanker, the *Probo Koala*, chartered by the Dutch energy firm Trafigura Beheer BV. Banny is due to set up a new cabinet that should include representatives of the political parties and the rebel *Forces Nouvelles* movement, as requested by the U.N.-backed peace process. According to Security Council Resolution 1633, adopted in October 2005, Banny is in charge of disarmament, identification and organising elections in October 2006. Gbagbo is allowed to remain in office for up to a year, on condition that the country holds 'free, fair, open and transparent' elections, and provided he works alongside Banny. On 27 September 2006, the head of the United Nations mission in Ivory Coast, Pierre Schori, announced that the country will not be able to hold presidential elections by the October 31 deadline since procedures for voter identification and registration are not firmly established.

Sport should not be relied upon miraculously to heal the gaping wounds dealt not by tusks but by *homo sapiens*, and to mend fences that no pachyderm can stand accused of trampling down, but some relaxation of tension was noted during June 2006 when, as well as Côte d'Ivoire, the adjacent Gulf states of Ghana and Togo qualified for the final stages of the soccer World Cup. Whether it is feasible, or even desirable, that a political candidate like George Weah, who ran Ellen Johnson-Sirleaf close in the 2005 Liberian presidential elections, could ever emerge from the ranks of foreign mercenaries such as Didier Drogba, Kolo Touré, Salomon Kalou, Emmanuel Éboué, Didier Zokora and Abdoulaye Meïté, to name but the ones plying their trade in the English Premier League, is not a supposition that should be dismissed out of hand. These are prestigious role models in a country that needs to be sustained by some hope. At the very least, success for new coach Uli Stielike's Elephants in the 2008 African Nations' Cup might produce a state of national euphoria capable of going some way towards soothing civil disorder and defusing xenophobic and sectarian hostility, as happened for a while in 'beur blanc rouge' France after the triumph of 1998.

Politics

Les Soleils des Indépendances may be interpreted as a parable for the progress of the soul. Part Three describes Fama's time of tribulation, when he is arrested, imprisoned, brought to trial and found guilty of treason. The narration, whose griot viewpoint is highly reflective of the Doumbouya family interests at stake in Part Two, returns to a greater degree of neutrality as Mariam and Fama travel back to the capital, this time in more comfort by train, with money provided by Balla and Diamourou.

Politics is the inspiration for *Les Soleils des Indépendances*, and will later receive sumptuous orchestration in *En attendant les retour des bêtes sauvages*. In this later novel, impressive CVs are rolled out for the three rival candidates for the presidency of the 'République du Golfe' (= Togo), yet they are all ousted by an uneducated former soldier (pp. 101-10). Koyaga, as fledgling ruler, visits Tiékoroni, the little man with the trilby hat whose totem is the cayman crocodile (clearly Houphouët-Boigny), and is told of the four 'méchantes bêtes', i.e. pitfalls of naïveté in *Realpolitik*, that any self-respecting dictator owes it to himself to avoid (pp. 193-204). Here, Machiavelli's *The Prince* is conflated with the art of the African fabulist. Later (pp. 241-8), the president of the 'République du Grand Fleuve' (= Mobutu) presents him to his four major political advisers, all shown by their potted biographies to be deeply corrupt.

Kourouma relates how the imprisonment of his friends in his home country of Côte d'Ivoire after the 'complot du chat noir' (an alleged animist sacrifice) was the event which prompted him to write the novel: 'Le premier, *Les Soleils des Indépendances*, c'était parce que j'avais des camarades qui étaient en prison. Il y avait une dictature qu'il fallait certainement dénoncer' (Ouédraogo, p. 773; *Quand on refuse*, pp. 86-87). Fama had previous 'form' when arrested, having (though, ironically, very much against his best interests) campaigned for the end of French colonial rule (**56-57**). He is taken first to the torture chambers in the grounds of the presidential palace (this is likely to be at Yamoussoukro [see *En attendant*, pp. 200-3 ; *Quand on* *refuse*, p. 86]), then to the nameless prison, and finally to Mayako barracks, where he is tried and where he spends his prison term before being released. The title of this section is significant in that, by not naming the prison camp, the author conveys the horror inspired by the camp and the regime that has authorised it, as well as the wish to insult the place and those who are responsible for it. The ultimate expression of contempt is not to recognise the existence of a person or an object by refusing to give it a name. The episode of Fama's arrest and imprisonment is important in terms of African history and sociology because the nameless prison evoked in the chapter title, 'Les choses qui ne peuvent pas être dites ne méritent pas de noms', is a place which exists to a more or less terrible degree in many African countries. Since leaders remain in power by eliminating or suppressing opposition, the prison and the torture chamber are a necessary part of the government's existence.

Fama's journey from the capital to his home village of Togobala, in the region of Worodougou, is an occasion for the telling of tales, the subject of which is the political situation since independence and how it has affected five individuals. Fama's fellow travellers are Diakité, Konaté and Sery, apprentice to the driver, Ouedrago. The *mise en abyme* of stories related by characters within a story is part of the oral tradition. The reader from an English background is reminded of Chaucer's *Canterbury Tales*.

In this case, the travellers' stories provide a commentary on the political situation in their different countries of origin. Kourouma's comic method is applied to show up the senselessness of totalitarian regimes, whether they are to the right or left of the political spectrum. Diakité's tale (**83-85**) is particularly effective in describing the bully-boy tactics of the members of the one-party socialist state in African countries. In African post-independence countries, such regimes suppressed private enterprise, particularly in neighbouring Guinea ('le Nikinai, c'était le socialisme'—**83**). Kourouma's political commentary in his novels is expressed via an individual's story which illustrates one person's experience of the regime. Diakité's father has everything taken from him: his livelihood, his son, his possessions. Humiliated by this treatment and driven to violence, he shoots dead five members of the party and rescues Diakité, who escapes through the night, before being brought to trial and shot. This salutary tale represents the propensity of many regimes to stoop to manipulation of the law, followed by limitless ferocity

The second passenger, Konaté, recounts his tale of escape from socialism (**85**). An exile, like so many others, he haunts the borders of his country, making a living from selling currency and articles on the black market. In other words, he has been reduced to smuggling, but tells his story and gives his opinions on politics in a roundabout fashion, anxious and comically adept at presenting himself as a hero rather than as a criminal. He is loth to criticise socialism directly, wary, the reader assumes, that his listeners may be members of the secret police:

> Konaté avait la nostalgie de son pays, il l'aimait, savait aussi que le socialisme après sera une bonne chose; mais comme pour tous les gros bébés, la naissance et les premiers pas étaient difficiles, trop durs [...]. C'était vraiment pour Allah, l'humanisme, le patriotisme, qu'il voyageait et cela en dépit de tous les risques qui guettent aux portes du socialisme. (**85**)

The third passenger, Sery, presents his crass, tabloid view of the solution to Africa's problems: everyone should stay in their own country (**85-88**). The young man is likened to a young wild animal and to a puppy, alerting the reader to the fact that his opinions are those of a very young and inexperienced boy. The naïve philosophy which he expounds is more harmful, however, than the humorous atmosphere suggests, as it is exactly these views which have led to internecine war in Africa. Such conflicts have caused as much destruction as the oppressive regimes which Kourouma satirises. This expression of unabashed xenophobia causes silence in the cab of the lorry : 'Il leva les yeux et tressaillit en s'apercevant que de tous côtés des regards de stupéfaction étaient fixés sur lui. Toutes les lèvres étaient tirées et tassées, les oreilles n'écoutaient que les soufflements du moteur' (**89**).

Kourouma's clipped style, involving enumeration ('quand arrivèrent l'indépendance, le socialisme et le parti unique'—**83**), vulgar embellishments (Diakité is attached to a tree by his penis) and satirical ventriloquism of pleonastic party slogans ('le socialisme était le socialisme!' [84], spouts the party official) combine to create an effect which is reminiscent of Shakespearean comedy.

More assimilable to Shakespearean tragedy is the notion of *gnamokodé (bâtardise)*. This Malinké word, used as an expletive by Birahima all the way through *Allah n'est pas obligé*, occurs early in the novel ('Fama se récriait: «Bâtard de bâtardise! Gnamokodé!» Et tout manigançait à l'exaspérer'—11), whereupon it is reiterated so often in French that it may be considered to be a major theme of the novel. The thinly fictionalised Côte / République des Ébènes, to recall Brutus's warning to the political conspirators of *Julius Caesar* (II, i), 'is guilty of a several bastardy'. This refers most often to the ruling party and the system of government installed in African countries since the colonial era; according to the traditional system of chieftainship, the presidency and government are illegitimate. Before independence, power was passed on from one generation to the next within the same family. The word *bâtardise* further encompasses all the Kafkaesque institutions of the one-party State, particularly the arbitrary nature of justice. Other references to *bâtardise* occur during Fama's tirades against the concept of state or nation. This relatively recent idea, again introduced by the colonial powers, is anathema to Fama. His rebellion against the nation state manifests itself verbally, but words are transformed into action when, in the final chapter, he crosses the bridge over the river separating the Côte des Ébènes from the République de Nikinai, falls from the bridge, is attacked by the sacred crocodile and dies of his wounds. This heroic act of defiance can be held to mark his triumph over the *bâtardise* which he has so long railed against, and Fama reaches the village of Togobala in what turns out to be his own funeral cortege:

> À partir de ce moment du texte, en effet, le personnage de Fama s'ennoblit et prend d'autres dimensions. Il avait été d'abord présenté sous un angle assez dérisoire. Mais cette résistance aux présages le rend, en somme, héroïque. (Borgomano, p. 95)

In terms of traditional beliefs, the natural order of life is turned upside down in the modern African state.

Kourouma makes a point which is also made by traditional healers, traditional chiefs and elders: that the present ills are brought about because the governments of post-independence Africa have neglected traditional practices, such as the appeasement of ancestral spirits through sacrifice, respect for the environment and for wild animals, and caring for vulnerable members of the family and community. To the Western reader, familiar with reasons such as the imbalance of conditions of trade, protectionism, corruption and ill-conceived aid projects, the word 'sacrifice' may bear no axiomatic relation to the political, social and economic problems experienced by African countries. These are, nevertheless, serious accusations, levelled at governments which should represent the people by the traditional healers and leaders of communities, whose present, nominal power has been passed from father to son or mother to daughter over many generations. Traditional practices, including rituals demonstrating respect for sacred places or for ancestral spirits, are symbolic of a sense of community, a regard for the weaker members of society: in short, of adherence to a moral code. Kourouma underlines the significance and consequences of this neglect, commencing with a reference to the two oracles of Togobala, the hyena and the serpent. The inhabitants of Togobala believe that a hyena and an ancient boa constrictor are the oracles of the village; the community spirit and mutual support embodied in the oracles are contrasted with the individualist approach of the city dweller and, especially, the politician:

> Où voyait-on le koma, l'hyène, le serpent ou le devin de la république des Ébènes? Nulle part. Il demeurait bien connu que les dirigeants des soleils des Indépendances consultaient très souvent le marabout, le sorcier, le devin; mais pour qui le faisaient-ils et pourquoi? Fama pouvait répondre, il le savait: ce n'était jamais pour la communauté, jamais pour le pays, ils consultaient toujours les sorciers pour eux-mêmes, pour affermir leur pouvoir, augmenter leur force, jeter un mauvais sort à leur ennemi. (**156-7**)

Chapter Three

Systems of belief

Islam and the Qur'an

In *Les Soleils des Indépendances*, Islam plays an important role because it is the religion of the Malinké people, descendants of the Mali empire (1235-1546). The first ruler of this, Maghan Sundiata, was a Muslim, who came from the Keita clan. The Mali emperor Mansa Moussa made a famous pilgrimage to Mecca with a gold-laden retinue of eight thousand in 1324. Islam is thought to have first come to West Africa through traders travelling from the Middle East to Ghana. In conformity with Kourouma's intention to write about the culture and traditions of his people, the Malinkés, he deals with a religion that forms a large part of their history, has enormous significance in the lives of the characters, and colours the themes of the novel. It can be safely contended that the author's knowledge of the Qur'an has influenced the structure and style of his writing.

Islam is a monotheistic religion, which dates from approximately 620 A.D. The Qur'an or Koran, the Holy Book of Islam, contains the revelations made to the prophet Mohammed on Mount Hira by Allah, through the angel Gabriel. Mohammed was made to recite the verses of the Qur'an in order to learn them, because he was illiterate. In keeping with the origins of the Holy Book, most Muslims learn portions by heart to use in daily devotions and many learn to recite the whole Qur'an. Those who can do this are called 'hafiz' and are believed to acquire grace through recitation. The emphasis on orality in *Les Soleils des Indépendances* stems from the tradition of West African storytelling but may also be related to the fact that in Muslim religious practice the emphasis is more on recitation than reading. The power of the word is a cultural as well as religious phenomenon, reflected in the frequency of pious phrases quoted by the characters and the narrator, to explain or justify actions or events and to provide comfort through the many trials of daily life. Fama, in quietening the professional mourners of Togobala, refers to the Qur'an to support his actions and decisions:

> Quelques instants après, le tourbillon avait passé, les pleureuses se précipitèrent pour reprendre. «Non et non! Allah dans son livre interdit de pleurer les décédés.» Pas de cris! Plus de lamentations! (**104**)

It also embellishes his interior monologue, for example in describing Mariam's beauty: 'Disons-le, parce que Allah aime le vrai!' (**129**).

The Qur'an specifies five Pillars of Islam: *Shahadah*, the Declaration of Faith; *Salat*, prayer; *Zakat*, almsgiving; *Sawm*, fasting during Ramadan; *Hajj*, pilgrimage to Mecca (see **140**). *Salat* is preceded by ritual washing and is performed at certain times of the day, regulated by the sun rather than the time, notably sunrise, noon, mid-afternoon, sunset and just after dark. Men are encouraged to go to the mosque to pray and women usually pray at home or in a separate gallery at the mosque. For example, Salimata prays at home, whereas Fama attends the mosque: 'Fama était parti à la mosquée, il y priait chaque matin son premier salut à Allah' (**45**). By giving a share of the food she sells to the beggars in the market, Salimata is performing *Zakat*, which requires Muslim traders to give 2.5% of the value of their goods to the needy.

The central event of Islam is death and resurrection. The ritual surrounding death in *Les Soleils des Indépendances* originates partly in the Muslim tradition and partly in the animist tradition of the Malinké people. Muslims believe in life after death; that the soul is carried to Allah by an angel; and that the person will be judged according to their deeds, going consequently to either heaven or hell. The ceremony of the seventh day, referred to in the novel (**10; 196**), is part of Muslim practice. Seven days after the burial, relatives return to the grave to pay their respects. The narrator of *Les Soleils des Indépendances* points out that the ceremony of forty days after a burial is a Malinké custom:

> Pourquoi les Malinkés fêtent-ils les funérailles du quarantième jour d'un enterré? Parce que quarante jours exactement après la sépulture les morts reçoivent l'arrivant mais ne lui cèdent une place et des bras hospitaliers que s'ils sont tous ivres de sang. (**138**)

The doctrine of predestination, drawn from Islam, is an integral part of Fama and Salimata's religious belief. Salimata refers to this doctrine after a long meditation on her sterility:

> ... et lorsque le jour tomba elle comprit Allah, convint de son sort. Elle avait le destin d'une femme stérile comme l'harmattan et la cendre. Malédiction! Malchance! Allah seul fixe le destin d'un être. (**32**)

The novel relates the final years of Fama's life as the last of his line, predestined to die without offspring and to fulfil the prophecy that the family would die out because of the disobedient act of an ancestor. It should be noted, however, that the prophecy is unrelated to Muslim belief; it is part of the history and culture of the family, as underlined by the protagonist's first name. The name, Fama, relates directly to the earliest history of the Mali empire, as it is the word for 'ruler' used to refer to the leader of a group of people, while the word *mansa* means *fama* of *famas* or leader of leaders.

In the first two parts of the novel, Fama's resolve in the face of practical difficulties, based on his religious faith, shows through:

> ... il ne lui reste qu'à attendre la poignée de riz de la providence d'Allah en priant le Bienfaiteur miséricordieux, parce que tant qu'Allah résidera dans le firmament, meme tous conjurés, tous les fils d'esclaves, le parti unique, le chef unique, jamais ils ne réussiront à faire crever Fama de faim. (**25**)

> —Merci! À tous, merci! Que tombent et la bénédiction et la reconnaissance d'Allah sur tous les prometteurs de tant de soins, de protection et d'humanité! (**115**)

Animism

Animism, according to the *Encyclopedia Britannica*, is the belief in innumerable spirit beings, who are concerned with human affairs and capable of helping or harming men's interests. In some societies, totemism and the cult of ancestors form part of animistic belief, as they do in *Les Soleils des Indépendances*. Animistic creeds have in common an undertaking on the part of men to communicate with supernatural beings about the practicalities of everyday life, securing food, curing illness, averting danger and, in the case of Salimata, inducing fertility. Another element of animism is the belief in the spirit double. For instance, Balla interprets a nightmare of being attacked by vultures and grey lizards as follows: 'Le double, le dja de Fama avait quitté le corps pendant le sommeil et avait été pourchassé par les sorciers mangeurs de doubles' (**119**).

Animism attributes importance to categories or groups of supernatural beings, whose individual members are attached to particular places and persons, or resident in particular creatures. In such a system, each human encounter must work itself out as a distinct episode; Christianity and Islam are known as hierarchical religions compared to animism, because followers are told what to believe and how to act by a central power, whereas animist beliefs vary from one society to another. Each community makes its own adaptations which are particular to their environment.

The beliefs portrayed in the novel involve a world animated by numerous spirits, represented in trees, plants, birds, animals, celestial bodies and winds. Besides these esteemed spirits, there are other malevolent spirits: ghosts, restless spirits of ancestors treated improperly after death, monsters and demons, like the one said to have taken possession of Salimata and whose jealousy is responsible for all the ills which befall her (**73**). Animism encourages man to ward off such troubles by observing taboos and respecting a set of rules governing behaviour; once trouble is encountered, the diviner is enlisted to identify the demon or disgruntled spirit and propose ritual cleansing, propitiation or sacrifice. However, to demonstrate Kourouma's satirical purpose, the witch doctor Balla is blind (**110**).

The tall tales told by hunters, in which supernatural, credulity-defying metamorphoses occur, may be reminiscent of those told to young Ahmadou Kourouma by his father Moriba. Balla's exploits as a younger man are presented as an invitation to listen—'Comment

Balla devint-il le plus grand chasseur de tout le Horodougou?' (**122**)—that could hardly be declined. Thanks to the local equivalent of a pact with the devil, a bargain struck with the hunter genie, Balla always hunts down and kills as much prey as he wishes, to the extent that he becomes, with the help of his griot's embroidery of his deeds (**123**), a crashing bore. The 'combat [...] épique' (**124**) with the spirit of the buffalo, during which, by successive transformations, they seek to neutralise one another in a cosmic 'rock, paper, scissors' combat, turns out to Balla's advantage, but an unspecified payback time, when the tables will be turned and the hunter slaughtered by the genie, seems fast approaching. He survives by identifying, aided by 'marabout, féticheurs et sorciers' (**125**), the *kala*, or Achilles heel, of the genie, and blows it to smithereens with a hefty charge of gunpowder spiked with water-deer droppings, after which he puts his gun and his traps away for good. A series of similar epic encounters occurs in *En attendant le vote des bêtes sauvages* (pp. 69-73), when Koyaga kills a lone panther, a black buffalo, an elephant and a sacred cayman, stopping their evil spirits, or *nyamas*, from roaming abroad by stuffing their tails into their mouths, just as later he will do with the manhood of any political adversary he is forced to kill.

The profession of Diamourou, the faithful family retainer (**107**), is the secular one of griot, one who recites the genealogy and history of his people, but he is also a devout Muslim, who calls upon Allah and refers to His word ('Louange à Allah!'—**109**; 'se souvenant des paroles du Coran'—**108**). Against him is set the evil-smelling Balla, the *féticheur*, whose practices are inspired by animist beliefs and are repugnant to the narrator: '(nous viderons dans la suite le sac de ce vieux fauve, vieux clabaud, vieille hyène)' (**105**). In a somehow intermediate position is situated the 'marabout sorcier' Abdoulaye (**65**), one of the holy priests of the Muslim religion, always ready with a timely and inspiring word: 'Les volontés d'Allah et des saints ont été faites' (*ibid.*); 'Un malheur définitivement détourné! Louange à Allah! Salimata méritait cette faveur, son humanité, sa foi, sa charité étant sans limite' (**72**). The *marabout* of West Africa has another role, however; Abdoulaye is born in the magical place of Timbuktu (**65**; Gassama, pp. 87-88) and he is also a magician, diviner and spirit medium, who predicts the future and wards off misfortune. By declaring to Salimata: 'Allah a sacré le mariage, c'est un totem' (**76**), Abdoulaye demonstrates the concomitant existence of Islam and animism in the society of Côte d'Ivoire that is portrayed in the novel.

Diamourou is hostile towards Balla, who in addition to bearing the stigma of being descended from a slave, has rejected Islam in favour of animism: 'Un Cafre de la carapace de Balla dans un village d'Allah comme Togobala! Un féticheur, un lanceur de mauvais sorts, un ennemi public d'Allah, alors! Alors!' (**111**), with the word 'Cafre' (Kaffir) being taken in the restricted, pejorative sense of 'pagan'. However, Diamourou should perhaps not be casting the first stone: there are skeletons in his own family cupboard, for he has prospered as the result of a kind of 'mariage-rapt' of his daughter Matali by a white man.[1] On Fama's return to Togobala, the narrator, from a standpoint of loftier omniscience, comments on the differences between the two systems of belief, which exist side by side:

> Le musulman écoute le Coran, le féticheur suit le Koma, mais à Togobala, aux yeux de tout le monde, tout le monde se dit et respire musulman, seul chacun craint le fétiche. Ni margouillat ni hirondelle! (**105**)

This is why holy men like Abdoulaye are pragmatic enough to dabble in witchcraft. The tension between animist and Muslim beliefs is portrayed, but in enterprises of great pitch and moment the two systems work together, for example to support Fama against the single party's takeover bid for the traditional chieftainship.

Lineage

Fama's bumptious, though increasingly embattled, self-confidence, stems from his powerful belief in the prestige of his family line. Just

---

[1] Diamourou discloses to Fama (**107-9**) the story of his daughter Matali's forced concubinage with a local police chief, and the continuing support he receives from her and 'mes deux mulâtres de petits-enfants', now high-ranking officials. There is material here for the kind of *conte leste* that Maupassant would have gone to town on, as in *L'Ami Patience*, which tells of how a brothel is started up with a man's wife and sister-in-law, and indeed much greater similarities to Zola's *Jacques Damour*.

as Joseph was 'of the house and lineage of David' (Luke, II, 4), he is of the house and lineage of Moriba (**97**), whose shade has to witness Fama's humiliation (**17**). He is a member of the Malinké people, who originate from the north-western corner of the Côte d'Ivoire. These people are members of the Mandé group, inheritors of a culture made famous from the 13th to the 16th centuries by the Mali empire. Long before then, the Mandés had effected a regional agricultural revolution, discovering the use of millet ('fonios'—**113**), which remains their staple food. They have cultivated cotton for centuries. Cattle are kept by everyone, but for purposes of prestige and use on ceremonial occasions rather than for economic reasons. The men raise livestock, cultivate crops and also travel extensively for trade. Fama blames the degeneration of the economy on the socialism of the ruling party, which has ruined opportunities for commerce: 'La colonisation a banni et tué la guerre mais favorisé le négoce, les Indépendances ont cassé le négoce et la guerre ne venait pas' (**23**).

As we have seen in the preceding section, Kourouma's writings have an important historical dimension, none more so than his second novel, *Monnè, outrages et défis* (1990), which may be described as a historical novel. The third novel, *En attendant le vote des bêtes sauvages* also provides an historical account, but of more recent events. Kourouma is quite clear about his enterprise in writing fiction. He wishes to provide an account of African history, because there is a lack of balance in historical accounts to date, the story of colonialism not having been told from the African's point of view:

> Quant à *Monnè, outrages et défis*, je suis toujours choqué de constater que de la colonisation on n'en parle pas, les morts de la colonisation on n'en parle pas, les morts de l'esclavage on n'en parle pas. Tous les jours, on nous dit ce que le communisme a commis comme crimes. En France, ils parlent tout le temps de l'occupation de quatre ans. Ils en parlent depuis combien d'années? Cela fait cinquante ans qu'on en parle. Et nous, on n'en parle pas. C'était un peu, pour répondre à cette question, pour dire que nous aussi on a souffert. (Ouédraogo, pp. 773-4)

The question of family history is raised in the early part of *Les Soleils des Indépendances* at the funeral palaver by Fama's insistence on his dynasty, but the issue is treated with more seriousness once Fama is completely alone on his long journey back to Togobala. For the first time, he begins to take responsibility for his situation and considers his position in this disconcertingly transformed and constantly changing world: 'Et Fama commença de penser à l'histoire de la dynastie pour interpréter les choses, faire l'exégèse des dires afin de trouver sa propre destinée' (**97**). The return to the source, to the earliest known history, supports the protagonist's attempt to know his authentic nature, to turn away from bombast and bragging in an effort to understand himself, and to reconcile himself to his destiny. By examining the past, he discovers that the greed of an ancestor has led to the line dying out. The allegorical tale may be interpreted as a moral lesson, in terms of 'reaping what you sow'. The fictional tale imparts morality: Fama traces his ancestry to a certain Souleymane Doumbouya, whose lineage prospered until the conquest of the land of Worodougou by the Malinké Muslims originating in the countries to the north of the present-day Côte d'Ivoire, in colonial times, French Sudan.[2] The ancestor Bakary, the descendant of Souleymane Doumbouya, collaborates with the enemy in exchange for retaining his power. Bakary is identified as the source of Fama's tragic destiny, committing the ultimate sin by throwing in his lot with the invaders in return for power. Collaboration also seals the destiny of the king of Soba, Djigui Keita, the central protagonist of *Monnè, outrages et défis*. Rather than comforting Fama, the return to the source only increases his fear, as he gradually comes to terms with his inexorable fate. This moral flaw is seen as the cause of Fama's sterility: his life story marks the end of the Doumbouya dynasty, a destiny brought about by the ancestor's being caught in no man's land.

Whilst emphasising the influence of history on the present, Kourouma acknowledges the fact that there are many versions of the same historical event, and indeed provides two derivations of the name Togobala. This recognition of diverse versions is apparent in

---

[2] In Yambo Ouologuem's *Le Devoir de violence* (Paris: Seuil, 1968, p. 82), a 'négrier soudanien' who drugs his unsuspecting victims goes by the name of Doumbouya.

III: Systems of belief

the conflicting accounts of Souleymane Doumbouya's arrival and founding of it (**97-98**). The second account is comic, proposing that the drunkenness of the ruler due to receive the visitor was the real reason behind Togobala's geographical location. Providing two or more versions of the same historical event is also a narrative technique whereby the reader is obliged to distance him or herself from the story and to consider the events from a broader angle.

When Fama returns to his home village for the occasion of his cousin Lacina's funeral, his physical presence represents his formal acceptance of the chieftainship of his tribe. Balla and Diamourou treat Fama as the saviour of his people, encouraging him to marry Mariam and produce the children who will ensure the future of the dynasty. There is constant narrative tension, therefore, between the intentions of the two normally hostile leaders of the community (in truth, there are but four men, only two of whom are able-bodied [**107**], and no married women of untarnished conjugal virtue to aid Balla in his efforts to cure ailing livestock [**130**]) and Fama's lack of conviction. The situation has a further, ironic dimension because of the dilapidated state of Fama's inheritance:

> Au soir de leur vie les deux vieillards [Diamourou and Balla] œuvraient à la réhabilitation de la chefferie, au retour d'un monde légitime. Malheureusement, Togobala, les Doumbouya et même le Horodougou ne valaient pas en Afrique un grain dans un sac de fonios. (**113**)

> La pauvreté ne se guérit pas, ne se dissimule pas à Togobala. (**127**)

His homeland is inhabited by a dispossessed people, deprived of their livelihood by the socialist policies of their leaders and a harsh climate and environment. Fama continues nonetheless to behave like a potentate, making courtesy visits to the smallholdings of his subjects, receiving petitions and settling disputes, encouraged and supported financially by Balla and Diamourou. The pomp and ceremony attached to his position come to a climax in the funeral ceremony and feasting surrounding it.

The humorous contrast between the ideal and the real is portrayed succinctly in the following sentence:

> Avec les pas souples de son totem panthère, des gestes royaux et des saluts majestueux (dommage que le boubou ait été poussiéreux et froissé!), en tête d'une escorte d'habitants et d'une nuée de bambins, Fama atteignit la cour des aïeux Doumbouya. (**103**)

The humour here and in other such examples has a serious intent. In this way, Kourouma poses the essential question of Africa's future. By properly recounting history and valuing traditional practices, the individual is sure of their identity and better prepared to cope and adapt to the demands of the present. In an increasingly technological world, which is dominated by the strong economies of the West, societies in African countries need to be sure of their value and confident enough to adapt and move forward in today's world. Fama and his lineage are anachronistic; future generations need not be so.

Faith-based daily life

a) The Muslim woman

If Fama is obsessed by family in the broad sense, and if the way in which his acts and gestures are narrated appears to reflect this belief system (see Chapter Five), Salimata, who is treated with more conventional narratorial omniscience, has a specific and narrower preoccupation with this same subject: she simply wants to be in the family way. She is a devout Muslim woman, wearing the traditional 'mouchoir de tête', though not the facescarf (**33; 63**), and less distracted in her religious devotions than Fama, though her attention has been known to stray from her prayers at times (**44**).

We see Salimata only in the capital city, where she has been forced to become the main hunter-gatherer of the couple. Without any education or formal training, she provides for the needs of the couple by selling pre-prepared food or by growing and selling vegetables or other products such as cloth. She has an agreeable

III: Systems of belief

personality as a market trader, although her bulk catering skills are perhaps but recently acquired, and uneven: 'La viande était coriace, mais la sauce était excellente et le riz un peu dur' (**57**). Fama, whom she sees as 'un vaurien comme une crotte' (**35**), 'inutile et vide la nuit, inutile et vide le jour, chose usée et fatiguée comme une vieille calebasse ébréchée' (**55**), is clearly of little more use than a chocolate fireguard; when she asks him, and the use of the participle is colourful and interesting, whether he will remain 'tout le long de ce grand soleil dispersé comme ça sur la chaise?' he ignores her, 'occupé à dénombrer les bâtardises des soleils des Indépendances' (*ibid.*) He can be relied upon to wash his own hands, but nary a plate (**57**).

Kourouma champions the cause of the African woman in a no-nonsense approach which condemns traditional practices like female excision and the inequality of women before the law. He uses the device of the refrain, which evokes Salimata's memory of her excision and subsequent rape by the traditional healer into whose care she is placed. This episode frequently invests Salimata's stream of consciousness, and is telescoped into one word, the proper name 'Tiécoura', to denote a rapist; needless to say, the double negative of 'Salimata ne savait pas si ce n'était pas le féticheur Tiécoura qui l'avait violée dans sa plaie d'excisée' (**39**) means that it was indeed he.

Through Salimata's story, Kourouma demonstrates his lack of nostalgia about pre-colonial Africa. Earlier writers, most notably Laye, tend to idealise traditional African society of these times. Kourouma has no such illusions and, by adopting Salimata's point of view, his novel indicates that male-dominated social structures, which are oppressive of women, must change in order to allow the individual African man or woman to achieve his or her full potential. This implied criticism is present in the irony of one short sentence, which summarises all that society expects of women and the little that is expected of men: 'Le mari était servi' (**57**).

The question of polygamy has received significant and serious literary treatment from Mariama Bâ in *Une si longue lettre*. Kourouma is perhaps the first male writer to treat the question from the point of view of the man. Fama knows that by making the journey to his cousin Lacina's funeral, not only will he take on the chieftainship of the Worodougou village but he will be required to take on the responsibility of Lacina's youngest wife, Mariam, promised to Fama before she married the late chief. However, Salimata's opposition to this union dominates Fama's thinking on polygamy, as he is only too aware of how miserable she will make his life if he takes on a second wife. Without defending the man's position, Kourouma subtly outlines the social pressures which are often brought to bear on the man, first to produce children, if need be by taking a second or third wife, second to take on the responsibility of a dead relative's family by marrying one or more of the widows.

Salimata is torn between *féticheur* and *marabout*. *Les Soleils des Indépendances* casts doubt on the usefulness of the traditional healer in African society. The reader may wonder whether Salimata's inability to conceive has to do with her excision—'trancher le clitoris considéré comme l'impureté, la confusion, l'imperfection' (36)—and rape in a still-scarred orifice when still an adolescent. She persists, nevertheless, in her hope for a child and spends all her money on 'cures'; her life is ruled by this one obsession. The implied criticism of the healers, who are happy to accept Salimata's money without being able to help her, as well as the fact that the problem was probably caused by a member of the animist branch of this profession, combine to suggest that this aspect of traditional African society is open to abuse. The reader is led to question the role of the healer, to wonder whether structures could be applied to monitor unethical practices and abuse of a position of authority.

The healers we encounter in *Les Soleils des Indépendances* are male; the figure of Abdoulaye, a *marabout*, provides another facet to the series of male figures who surround Salimata, within which she turns like a moth, making no progress but trapped by the attraction of the light, in her case the false hope sustained by these various characters. Abdoulaye is in love with Salimata, or at least entranced by her charms. She sweeps and cleans for him, in exchange for his predictions about the future, obtained through communication with the dead. The reader warms to him at times, yet he loses some of his dignity as a medium when he responds to some of the less ignorable attributes of the beautiful Salimata (72), who is herself not always

III: Systems of belief

above taking advantage of this situation. He has a vision of a terrible fate, which must be averted through the sacrifice of a cockerel. Salimata and he are poles apart in their interpretation of the sacrifice, as it is Salimata's memories of her excision and rape that are stirred by the blood. Abdoulaye tells her that Fama is sterile because he himself desires her, but she only sees her tormentor Tiécoura when she looks at him. Once he attempts to possess her, the dignified *marabout* is metamorphosed into a sexual predator. A near-farcical situation ensues as Salimata resists and attacks him with a knife, her fury and desire for vengeance for her rape taking over. The power passes with lightning speed from the *marabout* to the woman, who moments before was submissive and who is now transformed into a dervish, brandishing her knife and terrifying. The episode has a positive outcome as far as Salimata is concerned; her anger has put her in touch with the truth, and she now knows instinctively as she casts the bloody corpse of the rooster into the water that she will never have a child, though perhaps not by her fault.

In a sense, Salimata's efforts to enhance her fertility through the use of magic, potions and sacrifice are symbolic acts undertaken to purge and purify the act of excision and rape. There is a hint, at the end of the novel, that Salimata will at last respond to the advances of Abdoulaye and conceive because of the metamorphosis which has taken place in her husband. Fama leaves the capital, we are told, because there is no one there who loves him and wants to be with him after his period of imprisonment; Bakary's reasons are too self-interested, and are greeted with the Olympian disdain of a sadder and wiser man. The old Fama would have been bitter about this, but the new Fama recognizes that Salimata is a selfless, loving wife and that the best he can do for her, after all that she has suffered, is to give her her freedom:

> Ce qui avait arrêté Salimata ces derniers temps n'était ni l'amour, ni le caractère sacré du mariage, ni les longs souvenirs communs. Ce qui avait retenu Salimata prisonnière dans l'union était l'impossibilité pour elle de vivre avec un autre. Pour la première fois donc de sa vie, Salimata supportait un autre homme. Peut-être l'aimait-elle. Peut-être allait-elle avoir un enfant. Peut-être était-elle heureuse. Fama le souhaitait. Et pour

> que le bonheur de Salimata ne soit pas troublé, Fama avait le devoir de ne plus paraître dans la capitale où sa présence aurait été un continuel reproche moral pour Salimata. (**184**)

Salimata is the tragic heroine of *Les Soleils*, with all the dignity and courage of a Phaedra, eaten by her obsession but proud, strong, brave and compassionate. The male characters are all, at times, figures of fun, but Salimata provokes only the admiration of the reader. Empathy is generated by a narrative technique which moves smoothly into and out of her thoughts, presented as interior monologue in free indirect style. Consider this unostentatious, but very moving passage, character-based psychological focalisation as far as the exclamatory 's'y terrer!', to be followed by sentences that may veer towards third-person omniscient narrative, but which are couched in language straightforward enough to be Salimata's own. They deal with loss of face in the eyes of the community after her pregnancy has been revealed as a phantom one only, a humiliation that is perceived as being deserved by the woman alone:

> Ce qui est malheureux dans ce genre de choses, c'est la honte subséquente. Une honte à vouloir fendre le sol pour s'y terrer! Après des mois de grossesse, sans avortement, sans accouchement, il faut sortir comme les autres, voir et parler aux autres, et rire aux gens. Évidemment les questions égratignent et embarrassent les gorges des interlocuteurs, on le voit. Alors, chaque fois on devient quelque chose, quelque chose de différent qui craint tout le monde. (**53**)

Her meaningful presence in the novel fades away, hardly to return in more than the most episodic fashion, on the fatalistic note: 'Elle avait le destin de mourir stérile' (**78**). She is a victim of insufficient self-belief, i.e. low self-esteem, and it is Fama who now will move to the centre of the stage.

b) The Muslim man

The first two chapters of the novel describe Fama's daily routine in the capital. The centre of his world is religious life, particularly

III: Systems of belief

that related to the ritual of funeral. The rhythm of his life is dictated by the Muslim call to prayer and by his attendance at funerals, in his capacity as the last of the Doumbouya lineage of princes of Worodougou. In fact, Fama depends on the handouts disbursed at funerals to make his living. During the colonial era, Fama was a trader, a professional life followed traditionally by members of his Malinké people. The reader is told of his former life:

> Fama déboucha sur la place du marché derrière la mosquée des Sénégalais. Le marché était levé mais persistaient des odeurs malgré le vent. Odeurs de tous les grands marchés d'Afrique: Dakar, Bamako, Bobo, Bouaké; tous les grands marchés que Fama avait foulés en grand commerçant. (22)

It is not objectively clear exactly how influential and rich he was, since his fall is presented through his own, self-pitying thoughts 'Lui, Fama, né dans l'or [...]. Éduqué pour préférer l'or à l'or' (12), but this Dioula jeweller and dealer in precious metals—the proper name, like 'Cafre' (*supra*, p. 30) is taken in a more restricted sense than that of ethnic grouping—has travelled widely (22). No doubt, too, his wife did not have to work for a living, though if this is so she bears it with submissive resignation. Not so Fama; like Zola's idle parasite Auguste Lantier, whose former trade of *chapelier* is often substituted for his name in clear mockery of his inactivity, 'Son ancien titre de patron restait sur toute sa personne comme une noblesse, à laquelle il ne pouvait plus déroger' (*L'Assommoir*, ch. VIII).

There are five prayer times in the day of the Muslim, though some ambiguity in the references in this particular novel,[3] and Fama and Salimata regulate their daily activities around these. Fama hurries from the funeral to the mosque in the first scene of the novel. The reader discovers that, in addition to his 'charognard' ceremonial role as the last of the Doumbouya royal line (12), he has another one to

---

[3] There is no doubt whatsoever in any of Kourouma's later works, not even in Birahima's mind, about the e prayers and times (dawn, 13H00, 16H30, sunset, 20H00), but here, Salimata 'faisait l'aumône et les quatre prières journalières' (28), the fourth prayer is referred to almost as though it were the last (126), and it is not until the final reference to 'la cinquième prière' (135) that the confusion is dispelled. See also 45; 120, and particularly the mentions of *l'ourebi*, the third prayer (97; 98; 122; 133).

fulfil, as the muezzin at the mosque, before attending to his own prayers. Religious devotions provide a structure to the chaos of existence for both Fama and Salimata, and their belief in the power of the traditional healer sorts tolerably with their belief in Allah (**105**).

As Fama makes his way through the streets of the capital, which are teeming with life and all sorts of traffic, he curses the politicians, the Whites for colonising the country and the Blacks for allowing them to do so. Since 1950, Abidjan has doubled its population every six years, reaching 500, 000 in 1970. Urban planning has improved white areas whilst ignoring the needs of the majority of the population. Fama's critique of the present African political and social scenario is amusing and disturbing, and the reader is made aware of the ever-worsening situation from the point of view of this anti-hero.

In *Les Soleils des Indépendances*, the home village of Togobala is idealised by Fama. Already en route at Bindia he had luxuriated in 'l'ombre d'une nuit africaine non bâtardisée' (**95**), and he compares its calm, orderly rhythm, governed by the seasons, to the turmoil of the city streets, inhabited by malevolent lowlife that adds to the difficulties already encountered by Fama. In fact, Fama is in exile from his inheritance as leader of his people, for the colonial administrator of the province of Worogoudou preferred the more compliant cousin, Lacina, to the insolent and demanding rightful leader, Fama. And when he returns for the funeral, he must steer a canny course between the demands of the village elders and the civil authorities. Faithwise, because he is Malinké in wanting it both ways (**105**), if Salimata falls between *marabout* and *féticheur*, then Fama is caught between the rock and the hard place of *féticheur* and griot.

Part Three of *Les Soleils des Indépendances* contains fewer religious references. Fama's transformation from ne'er-do-well to prince in moral terms takes place, therefore, as an autonomous act undertaken alone, far from the public arena of the funeral or the mosque.[4] The context for this metamorphosis combines animist belief, faith in dynasty and in 'le dernier jugement d'Allah' (**170**; **185**). The

---

[4] A more heartfelt note is struck when a phrase first used to describe hia wife at prayer, 'elle [...] se livra à la bonne et réconfortante prière du matin' (**44**), is repeated in relation to Fama in prison: 'chaque matin il se réveillait avant les chants du coq pour se livrer à la bonne prière du matin' (**170**).

experience of torture and imprisonment seems to be the catalyst which makes Fama abandon his tendency to use religion as a scapegoat. He adopts a more mature position, that of the believer who internalises faith in certain doctrines and values and incorporates these into a personal system of belief. At this point, Fama takes on full responsibility for his life and accepts that his destiny will unfold in accordance with prophecy. Consequently, his actions in Part Three are performed beyond the framework of religious reference outlined in Parts One and Two.

As well as performing his duties at the mosque, Fama must carry out his conjugal ones, and impregnation of Salimata is at the top of the list. This 'corvée abominable', to quote Zola again (*Nana*, ch. XIII), performed by the older, less feisty husband on a woman reified by the partitive article, is a standard motif of ribald humour:

> Sur-le-champ, même rompu, cassé, bâillant et sommeillant, même flasque et froid dans tout le bas-ventre, même convaincu de la futilité des choses avec une stérile, Fama devait jouer à l'empressé et consommer du Salimata chaud [...]. (**30**)

Although for obvious physiological reasons her enjoyment does not hit some of the high spots, Salimata is an enthusiastic and sensual partner, who had eyes only for Fama from the first time she saw him (**48**). She had undertaken a dangerous journey to her chosen one in a nearby town, escaping the tyranny of arranged matches that first involved failed attempts at anatomical fine tuning with a strangulated hernia sufferer, then the threats of his surviving brother. Indeed, though her focalisation had better be accepted on the level of sentimental hyperbole alone: 'Elle aimait à l'avaler!' (**56**). Fama's chauvinistic thoughts on his wife's being a non-starter in the fertility stakes, or offensive suppositions such as 'Qui pouvait le rassurer sur la pureté musulmane des gestes de Salimata?' (**29**), do not stand up to close scrutiny. It is just possible that the shots at surrogate motherhood that motivate his visits—'(ô honte!)' interjects the narrator (**56**)—to the oldest professionals of Abidjan have resulted in a little Fama or two. But with such a transient population: 'D'ailleurs, elles ne pouvaient pas rester!' (*ibid*.), who knows? This sounds like face-saving on his part, for if any pregnancy had resulted he would no doubt have been reminded of this in no uncertain terms. On seeing Mariam, Fama is 'ranimé de la virilité d'un mulet' (**128**); but this comparison is double-edged, because just as size isn't everything, though it would certainly be a factor in the animal cross, *virilité*, for the always sterile mule and arguably by extension Fama, does not equate to *fécondité*.

What about male circumcision? According to a distinction made by Joseph Wambaugh (*The Choirboys*) that strays into the territory of West African animal metaphor—'anteaters' and 'helmets'—, Fama is clearly one of the latter. 'Incirconcis' and *bilakoro*, the Malinké word for wannabe adolescent, are terms of abuse and definition, respectively, in Kourouma's work. No doubt the operation took place in the traditional way, the day before Ramadan begins, at an event of the kind described by Camara Laye (*L'Enfant noir*, ch. VII). But if excision triggers in Salimata lifelong recurrent waking trauma, here, in reverse process, a dream recalls a ceremony of male bonding and pride: 'un de ces rêves qui vous restent dans les yeux toute la vie, qui vous marquent comme le jour de votre circoncision' (**163**), but not in a painful way.

Though the spotlight falls more on Fama than on Salimata, many of his pursuits can seem trivial when compared to her travails. His status of *inadapté* and his destiny result from miscalculations on his part. His fecklessness and his snobbishness stem from his over-inflated idea of his own importance. His destiny is sealed by the anachronistic nature of his aspirations. His behaviour is learned within a social structure which exalts the identity of the male at the expense of the female; in other words, most of what goes on in daily life, however daft at times, is strictly men's business.

Chapter Four

Language

In spite the long journeys undertaken, and epic trials and tribulations suffered by Fama and Salimata, it is not unreasonable to suggest that the biggest adventure in *Les Soleils des Indépendances* is one of language. The manuscript was rejected by French publishers and appeared initially in Canada. Kourouma's irreverent attitude towards the French language was unacceptable to metropolitan publishers; his style of writing changes the accepted rules of grammar, invents words, and employs a whole range of original images and expletives. His work has been said to 'abuse' language, whereas, at the other end of the spectrum, the spare, classical prose of another Malinké, Camara Laye, in *L'Enfant noir*, bears witness to obedient assimilation to francophone educational norms. This exuberant use of language is central to the writing under consideration here, and is the aspect of Kourouma's work which has excited most comment. The process of writing is best described as the Africanisation of French, whereby, like many of his fellow African writers, Kourouma uses the language of the coloniser to express his fictional world, but transforms that language by coinings and by restructuring grammar and locutions in accordance with the speech patterns, cadences and grammar of his native tongue, Malinké. The extent of its penetration in the former Manding lands to the north and west of the country is emphasised when the net must be cast wide to find an interpreter at Fama's show trial: 'Cet interprète improvisé devait être un Malinké de l'autre côté du fleuve Bagbê' (**167**), said river being in Sierra Leone, some four hundred kilometres from the western border of Côte d'Ivoire.

Kourouma's writing is, therefore, highly innovative and markedly more related to spoken than written form, reflecting an African fictional tradition in which at one time the novel did not exist as such. This section examines selected examples in order to indicate how the manipulation of the French language by the author results in literary effects which have a profound influence on the reader's perception of and reaction to the text. Such would include: use of tenses, where there may be a lack of aspectual fit between Malinké and French; invention of new words by using a verb in adjectival form or creating an opposite meaning to a verb by using a prefix; employment of a style of excess, in which a plethora of nouns, verbs, adjectives, past participles, infinitives and complements describes a sequence of events; use of imagery reflecting West African belief systems; widespread insertion of proverbs into the narrative to mark a pause or reinforce a didactic purpose; and last but not least, the use of gross and scatological vocabulary.[1]

Verbal incongruities

Makhily Gassama draws our attention to the first line of the novel 'Il y avait une semaine qu'avait fini dans la capitale Koné Ibrahima, ou disons-le en malinké : il n'avait pas soutenu un petit rhume…' (**9**), explaining that the Malinké word *abãna* may be translated by the French 'il a fini, il est fini, il est mort' (*La Langue d'Ahmadou Kourouma*, pp. 26-29). *Abãna* is an infinitive form which does not convey any notion of time. Kourouma, therefore, chooses the pluperfect tense and inverts the usual subject plus verb order of the French sentence. The emphasis on tense and, therefore, on time is reminiscent of the famous opening sentence of Proust's *Du côté de chez Swann*: 'Longtemps, je me suis couché de bonne heure.' Thus Kourouma opens his novel with an expression of time, followed by a verb, followed by a place, and finally by the subject of the verb. The verb 'finir' conveys a very different meaning to 'mourir'; 'finir' leads

---

[1] In this and the following sections, analyses draw on the study by Jean-Claude Nicolas (pp. 151-60) and on the work of the Senegalese critic Makhily Gassama, who goes more deeply into certain syntactical and morphological features of the Malinké language reflected in the text. Nicolas (p. 183) also quotes critic Richard Bonneau's *boutade* that Kourouma's language is 'apparemment le français'.

the reader to think about the life of the person coming to an end whereas 'mourir' is an act apart from life, self-contained rather than referring back to the life that has been lived. The use of the pluperfect tense rather than the perfect or past historic underlines completion and the sense of time. The author's awareness of the possibilities offered by the Malinké word and the ambiguity of transposition into French (after all, the preferred option of 'était mort' can be bisemous) becomes clear on the last page of the novel when the sentence 'Fama avait fini, était fini' reappears (**196**); the non-francophone may, in any case, hesitate between the auxiliaries *avoir* or *être* with respect to verbs such as *paraître* and *passer*.

The deliberate emphasis on tense in the first sentence, and on the concept of time in general, has the effect of preparing the reader for an introduction to a very different, perhaps unacceptable, system of beliefs, in accordance with which the material life of Koné Ibrahima, who has no other role in the novel, has come to an end, but the journey of his spirit, described in animistic terms, is only just beginning. I would suggest that the use of the pluperfect has the effect of introducing the reader to a new world, in which a very different set of references will be brought into play: notions of time and duration, notions of what is real and not real, notions of what constitutes the absurd are all disrupted by *Les Soleils des Indépendances* and the turning upside down of the conventions of the French language forms an important part of the overall ethos of the text.

Two examples will suffice to demonstrate the effects of sudden changes in tense: from imperfect or past historic, to pluperfect (*le plus-que-parfait duratif*), and then to present (Gassama, p. 32). As Salimata is fleeing Tiémoko and pauses to catch her breath, the unexpected change of tense indicates that this is a memory: 'Elle n'en pouvait plus, elle s'était arrêtée, quelque temps seulement, car aussitôt la brousse s'était ébranlée' (**47**). On the other hand, 'Quelque temps seulement' and 'aussitôt' imply urgency taking place in present time, which, in turn, leads the reader to expect a past historic or perfect tense. The resulting disorientation induces empathy with the character's state of mind and, at the same time, subtly reminds the reader that the Malinké sense of time combines past, present and future, extending to the afterlife. A second example is taken from Balla's hunting adventures: 'Chaque harmattan, Balla avait accumulé exploits sur exploits comme un cultivateur aligne des buttes' (**123**). Again, an expression of time leads one to expect the imperfect, but once more this is a memory. The effect of the disruption of tense is heightened by the generalised comparison of the hunter to the farmer, with the simile expressed in the present. The apparently conflicting tenses, in this case, shift the narrative to an extratemporal state by inserting a general reference, valid for all time, in what is known as the gnomic present.[2] In this latter respect we might look at the ending to a fine passage of mixed sensory impressions, and note how it leads on to a perfect-pluperfect tense sequence, where past historic-pluperfect might have been expected.

> ... et cette exhalaison des derniers restes des journées d'harmattan qui vous pénètrent jusque dans le bout du cœur et vous jettent dans les tam-tams des souvenirs de l'enfance, des grands jours, des sautes de l'histoire et des incertitudes de l'avenir. Brusquement l'appel à la prière a retenti. Un soleil avait fini. (**118**)

'Sautes de l'histoire' indeed, in tense use! Bearing in mind the fact that the author is at pains to convey a specifically African universe, unusual uses of them go hand in hand with the portrayal of a different, but equally valid, cosmology compared to that of the West.

Malinkisms, or African French parlance, in verb conjugation, sometimes problematising Western distinctions between transitive and intransitive, literal and figurative, or eschewing pronominals or factitives, occur from an early stage, in examples such as the following: 'tout manigançait à l'exaspérer' (**11**); '-Assois tes fesses [...]!' (**15**); 'refroidissez le cœur' (**16**); 'rythmait, battait, damait' (**29**); 'la nuit mal dormie' (**32**); 'osa demander à coucher Salimata' (**50**); 'L'homme à son tour hurla le fauve, gronda le tonnerre' (**77**); 'sortant de l'autre monde pour s'asseoir et boire les prières' (**116**); 'marcher un mauvais voyage' (**146**); 'Une intrigue tombera Nakou' (**164**); 'les hommes rebroussèrent' (**192**); 'et frapperont les funérailles' (**196**).

---

[2] Cf. Flaubert, *Madame Bovary*, III, 10: '... et le bois du cercueil, heurté par les cailloux, fit ce bruit formidable qui nous semble être le retentissement de l'éternité'.

Another evident feature is verbal ellipsis, as immediately at the beginning of the novel when the deceased Koné Ibrahima's shade rouses itself, hawking up phlegm, before getting on the move— 'Comme [*pour / il arrive chez*] tout Malinké, quand la vie s'échappa de ses restes, son ombre se releva, graillonna, s'habilla et partit' (**9**). It may be behavioural, sketching Salimata with deft economy: 'Décochement d'un petit sourire vite réprimé: jamais de sourire sur la peau de prière d'Allah' (**44**), or figuring in the heavily nominalised 'Gémissement d'étonnement et soumission de Salimata bouleversée' (**67**), or even be notational, in a passage of descriptive *écriture artiste*:

> Au large, seul maître et omniprésent, le soleil. Son éclat, ses miroitements sur l'eau et sa chaleur. Un peu, les piaillements du moteur, mouillés et essoufflés dans l'espace et se perdant dans les profondeurs des eaux... (**51-52**)

Finally, some of the verb inversions are highly expressive in their daring. The first below underlines the peppery *odor di femina* euphemised earlier (**29**; see *infra*, p. 54), and if the second will, in an uneducated woman, take nothing to do with the literary and poetic feminine plural of *amours*, then there are compensatory benefits:

> Ô chaude, étouffante, presque pimentée, l'atmosphère de la case! (**37**)

> Éteints et consumés les amours que Fama et Salimata avaient l'un pour l'autre à cette époque! (**56**)

> Cent fois piteux Fama devait leur paraître! (**116**)

Neologisms

Gassama describes what he refers to as Kourouma's grammatical gymnastics in taking a noun and changing it into a verb, or inventing a different noun to indicate an activity rather than a person. The word *marabout* in West Africa means a holy man in the Muslim tradition; he is also a healer or magician, sometimes a mystic. In North Africa the *marabout* designates a saint or a hermit. The verbs 'marabouter' and 'démarabouter' are examples of Kourouma's technique of inventing neologisms. The word 'maraboutage' means the activities of the *marabout*—casting spells, foretelling the future or bringing misfortune to a person—as well as plotting (**23**). The neologism 'démarabouter' describes the sun gradually emerging from cloud in the sentence 'le soleil avait réussi à se dépêtrer, à se démarabouter' (**163**), implying that the mystery of the sun as it is veiled by cloud disappears once it comes into full view. Kourouma takes a word and reinvents it in a way which is disorientating but which makes his reader think creatively and positively about the new usage. The inventions are part of a ludic system of language adopted by the author to enliven his text, but also as a process which encourages questioning and originality in the thought process.[3]

Some neologisms are onomatopoeic renditions of bird calls ('bubulements des hiboux [...,] tutubements des chouettes', *nuance*!—**118-9**), some are gross ('dévulver' [**130**], hardly located by search engines since, is found with relief to be intransitive), and the occasional one is welcomely chaste ('contrebander' [**85**] referring to smuggling and not to detumescence). Others serve to convey a particularly emotive content, frequently where the author wishes to condemn a particular practice or feature of government or society. The tragedy of the girls who die during the excision ceremony and never return to their village is one such example, conveying the intensity of emotion in the participial adjectives invented from the verbal forms 'non retournées' and 'non pleurées' (**36**; see Gassama, p. 47). These terms suggest that the crime of womanslaughter is sanctioned by a set of social rules which would make it inappropriate for the family of the girl to protest at her death. The succinct form of words is more effective than paragraphs of text in an essay on the barbarism of this particular traditional practice.

Of a day when cloud affords welcome relief from the sun's fierce heat, the reader is told that: 'Le matin était patate douce' (**161**). Unattested elsewhere, this expression is charming in its simplicity.

---

[3] Gassama (p. 90) points out that the verb 'politiquer' in West African usage can be employed transitively in the sense of 'tromper', to trick.

The style of excess

One striking aspect of the style of *Les Soleils des Indépendances* is the lists of words used to describe an event or a person when one or two is considered sufficient by writers of French within the dominant cultural writing mode (if not, historically, by Rabelais). Various effects are created by the device of enumeration, creating the impression of vitality as an important characteristic of the world in which we are immersed. Despite the poverty, waste, degeneration and absurdity of life in post-independence Africa, there is an undeniable life force, present even in the horrific attack on Salamata by the very beggars she assists (**62-63**). Life refuses to give up; even those at the very bottom of the food chain rise up against the person who is only slightly more able than they are, in an attempt to live, to obtain, by any means necessary, the chance of survival. Another effect is to reify the character being described, underlining the fact that the author demonstrates little sympathy for his characters (Gassama, p. 55). By making a list of misfortunes, such as 'c'était [*sic*] l'excision, le viol, la séquestration, le couteau, les pleurs, les souffrances, les solitudes, toute une vie de malheur' (**47**), the reader or author is distanced from the character's troubled life.

Enumerations of verbs and verbal expressions reflect the hyperbole of the epic, for example in the seductive dance of a 'sex me here' Salamata: 'elle rythmait, battait, damait; le sol s'ébranlait, elle sautillait, se dégageait, battait des mains et chantait' (**29**); in Diamourou's account of his daughter's flight from the passionate commander of the colonial forces: 'Elle se refusa, lutta, bouscula gardes et portes, s'enfuit et disparut dans la brousse' (**108**); or in the following portrayal of the chattering classes of the country:

> Ils s'étaient tous enrichis avec l'indépendance, roulaient en voiture, dépensaient des billets de banque comme des feuilles mortes ramassées par terre, possédaient parfois quatre ou cinq femmes qui sympathisaient comme des brebis et faisaient des enfants comme des souris. (**158**)

Enumerations of nouns and subject complements can convey the steamrollering effect of political change:

> La colonisation, les commandants, les réquisitions, les épidémies, les sécheresses, les Indépendances, le parti unique et la révolution sont exactement des enfants de la même couche, des étrangers au Horodougou, des sortes de malédictions inventées par le diable. **(132)**

Equally, the importance of Fama in the eyes of the villagers of Togobala and the burlesque behavioural aspects of his role are conveyed by the list of nouns which debunk the solemnity of the occasion, creating a comic effect:

> Le Fama accroupi en boubou blanc était un homme de grande responsabilité, ayant d'importants devoirs: il avait à prolonger la dynastie, à faire prospérer Togobala et tout le Horodougou. Les fatalités, le destin, le sort, les bénédictions, les volontés et les jugements derniers d'Allah descendaient, se superposaient, se contredisaient. **(116)**

Enumerations of infinitives and past participles are common, giving vivid impressions, respectively of touchy paranoia or hectic activity such as the following: 'Fama, couché et repu, s'était vautré sur la natte, prêt à dégainer pour sabrer, faucher et vilipender la bâtardise' **(95)**; 'Dès le premier matin, elles avaient pilé, attisé les feux des foyers, posé, descendu et reposé les canaris' **(140)**.

Enumerations of object complements would include these vivid examples, the first involving synaesthesia, the exploitation of sensory perceptions of a different order, and the second, zeugma, the 'yoking together', i.e. association, of, say, the physical and the psychological (cf. 'Vêtu de probité candide et de lin blanc' [Hugo, 'Booz endormi']):

> Salimata n'oubliera jamais le rassemblement des filles, la marche à la file indienne dans la forêt, dans la rosée, la petite rivière passée à gué, les chants criards des matrones qui encadraient et l'arrivée dans un champ désherbé, labouré, au pied d'un mont dont le sommet boisé se perdait dans le brouillard et le cri sauvage des matrones indiquant «le champ de l'excision». **(35)**

> Elle venait le [Abdoulaye] consulter en se couvrant de parures, de sourires, d'yeux brillants et curieux. **(67)**

Adjectival enumerations would include the following example of no doubt feasible Malinké but certainly unpunctuated, fractured French—'C'était une vraie inconfortable et très dangereuse situation' (**132**)—and there are numerous exclamatory litanies of Fama's griefs. When description shades into character focalisation, as here, we are obviously entering the territory of narrative:

> Le ciel demeurait haut et lointain sauf du côté de la mer, où de solitaires et impertinents nuages commençaient à s'agiter et à se rechercher pour former l'orage. Bâtardes! déroutantes, dégoûtantes, les entre-saisons de ce pays mélangeant soleils et pluies. (**12**)

Proverbs and precepts

In addition to a slew of idiomatic expressions starting as early as the first sentence—'avait fini [...] ou disons-le en malinké: il n'avait pas soutenu un petit rhume...' (**9**)—, and which can elsewhere be fed back with devastating effect,[4] proverbs occur with great frequency in the text. These *sentences* (a significant *faux ami* in French, derived from the Latin *sententiæ*) have a dual purpose, related to the oral traditions of fable and storytelling. One of the objectives of the traditional storyteller is to teach his audience a moral or practical lesson, so the proverb is didactic. The second purpose of the proverb is to act as a mnemonic device, i.e. the audience is reminded of the sequence of events. The didactic content confers the status of teacher on the storyteller, from the listener's point of view.

The proverbs featuring here are illustrative of the cultural exoticism of the Malinké mind-set. If it is rare that there can be exact transcoding of idioms or proverbs from one European language to another,[5] then it is hardly surprising to experience a greater shock of the unexpected in *Les Soleils des Indépendances*. Tony D'Souza tells of

---

[4] The local idiom for bribery, 'mouiller la barbe', is also '«parler français»' (*En attendant*, p. 244)!

[5] To take a few examples: 'donner le tournis à qqn.' = the physiological nonsense of 'give s.o. twisted blood'; 'Faire contre mauvaise fortune bon cœur' = 'Grin and bear it'; 'Plaie d'argent n'est pas mortelle' = 'It's only money'; 'Un clou chasse l'autre' = 'Fight fire with fire'; 'Qui aime bien châtie bien' = the more graphic 'Spare the rod and spoil the child'.

how he 'went native' to the extent of being able to fashion creditable Worodougou proverbs (*Whiteman*, pp. 236-7), but he is very much, if the obvious expression be cited, the exception that proves the rule.

In *En attendant le vote des bêtes sauvages*, the griot Bingo embellishes his praise-song (*donsomana*) to the République du Golfe dictator Koyaga with the obligatory leavening of homespun maxims; it must, though, be admitted that these decorative analogies are usually verbal flourishes, less central to the unfolding plot than they are in *Les Soleils des Indépendances*. Fama is less practised than the griots at this art, and hence must rack his brains at the funeral gathering for the right things to say: 'il baissa la tête pour penser et renouveler les proverbes' (**14-15**). When he manages to figure out one that, though feeble, is perhaps receivable as a plea in his defence at the trial— '«Écoutez ce proverbe bien connu: l'esclave appartient à son maître; mais le maître des rêves de l'esclave est l'esclave seul»' (**166**)—, the judge gives him no chance to rehearse it. The third-person narrator of the novel is, as one might expect, vastly more accomplished in this domain, and we note the presence of a prudently vague apologia for revolt that can seem to be of universal applicability—'Toute puissance illégitime porte, comme le tonnerre, la foudre qui brûlera sa fin malheureuse' (**99**)— and one that rises to the universality of La Rochefoucauld's 'Le soleil ni le mort ne se peuvent regarder fixement'. This latter, 'La suprême injure qui ne se presse pas, ne se lasse pas, ne s'oublie pas, s'appelle la mort' (**81**), also happens to be seminal to Kourouma's West African *Weltanschauung*, reformulable as 'La mort, c'est l'ultime *monnè*', i.e. the last of a series of heaped-on humiliations that are the substance of his second novel. '[D]ans quelle réunion le molosse s'est-il séparé de sa *déhontée* façon de s'asseoir?' (**19**), including the italicised archaism, could be a Malinké formulation in reverse of 'bon sang ne saurait mentir' / 'the cream always rises to the top'. Others are based on the seasons and the winds, reflecting the natural local environment, as when Fama's state of numbed apathy after being released from imprisonment is conveyed by: 'Que la récolte du sorgho de l'harmattan prochain soit bonne ou mauvaise, le mourant s'en désintéresse' (**187**). A chapter heading such as 'Les choses qui ne peuvent pas être dites ne méritent pas de noms' (**151**), beyond being a proairetic 'trailer' on the level of advance plot summary,[6] is a proverbial formulation in its own right.

The frequent references to the moral teachings of the Qur'an, coming from the viewpoint of narrator or, frequently, protagonist, strengthen the validity of the story, remind the listener of the importance of the person via whom it is being recounted, and further serve to stress the theme of destiny which pervades the novel. They may be simple didactic analogies tinged with local colour—'La prière comportait deux tranches, comme une noix de cola' (**27**)—or a more intricately developed pearl of the faith:

> Allah a fabriqué une vie semblable à un tissu à bandes de diverses couleurs: bande de la couleur du bonheur et de la joie, bande de la couleur de la misère et de la maladie, bande de l'outrage et du déshonneur [the *monnè* once more]. (**22**)

There is a sense of personal commitment and obligation—

> Un voyage de cette espèce cassait l'échine d'un homme de l'âge de Fama. Mais que pouvait-il? Aller aux funérailles d'un cousin est commandement des coutumes et d'Allah. (**92**)

—and a woman such as Salimata must draw on Muslim teachings to sugar the bitter pill of her harsh life: 'La soumission de la femme, sa servitude sont les commandements d'Allah' (**45**). Fama might consider sleeping with Mariam on the creaky *tara* while his better half is out at her market pitch during the day, but: 'Il ne le fit pas; la coutume l'interdisait' (**153**). The chapter heading 'Où a-t-on vu Allah s'apitoyer sur un malheur?' (**58**), to be more fully orchestrated in Kourouma's fourth novel, *Allah n'est pas obligé*, rationalises the despicable mugging of a poor rice vendor who was only trying to exercise practical charity, an everyday trial that must be borne by Salimata with moral resilience and resignation.

Kourouma's characters are illiterate, and rely on proverbs to express beliefs and cultural practices, to comfort them in the face of reality, to assist in everyday communication. Nobody understands

---

[6] See *infra*, p. 70 and n. 5, and **159** to find this sentence repeated.

this better than crafty local president Babou, who begins speaking to the Togobala villagers with cautious humility before demonstrating the common touch required at the hustings as he launches into some well-rehearsed shtick larded with proverbs and couthy aphorisms. The reader is spared all of these except the dodgy grammar of 'L'humanisme et la fraternité sont avant tout dans la vie des hommes', but is let off the hook, although reminded that: '(tout le dire en était truffé)' (**134**).

Gross and scatological expressions

A pithy remark such as 'À renifler avec discrétion le pet de l'effronté, il vous juge sans nez' (**14**) is situated on the cusp between proverb and good, honest, earthy vulgarity. Gassama comments on the extensive use of expletives in the work of Kourouma, explaining that pornographic and scatological literature is popular in West African culture (and, as we are aware, in Chaucerian medieval literature). Expressions such as *gnamokodé*, for 'bastardy',[7] already to the power of two (cf. 'le bordel au carré'—*Allah*, p. 171) when first voiced—'«Bâtard de bâtardise! Gnamakodé!»' (**11**)—have a number of effects. Firstly, vulgarities are amusing and provide comic relief to the overriding feeling of hopelessness in members of African society during these sunofabitches of *Indépendances*; they build in frequency towards the end of the novel, reflecting perhaps the way Fama becomes increasingly bewitched, bothered and bewildered by the turn of events. Decorum reigns in an early euphemism for the *gnoussou-gnoussou* of Salimata—'les fumées montaient dans le pagne et pénétraient évidemment jusqu'à l'innommable dans une mosquée, disons le petit pot à poivre, à sel, à piment, à miel' (**29**)—but is soon statistically to be overwhelmed by locutions that more directly, and often amusingly, call a spade a spade:

---

[7] Literally, 'son of the bushes or the forest', implying that conception has occurred in the bushes and therefore out of wedlock (Gassama, p. 107). In the two child-soldier novels, Birahima will give increasingly inventive glosses, ending with 'Gnamakodé (putain de ma mère)!' (*Quand on refuse*, p. 133).

IV: Language   55

«Mes dires ont donc sonné le silence comme le pet de la vieille grand-mère dans le cercle des petits-enfants respectueux» [...]. (**95**)

Un bâtard [...] osa, debout sur ses deux testicules [*sic*], sortir de sa bouche que Fama étranger ne pouvait pas traverser sans carte d'identité! (**101**)

[L]a grande case commune, où étaient mis à l'attache les chevaux, ne se souvenait même plus de l'odeur du pissat. (**107**)

[U]ne puanteur comme l'approche de l'anus d'une civette [...]. (**110**)

Togobala, faut-il le redire, était plus pauvre que le cache-sexe de l'orphelin. (**127**)

[I]intraitable comme un âne nouvellement circoncis. (**127**)

«Pour qu'on t'appelle grand coureur, il faut en avoir un qui se lève devant.» (**130**)

Il ne pesait pas plus lourd qu'un duvet d'anus de poule. (**133**)

[L]es femmes propres devenaient rares dans le Horodougou comme les béliers à testicule unique. (**134**)

[T]oujours indomptable comme le sexe d'un âne enragé. (**135**)

[C]ela était aussi infaisable que manger les crottes d'un chien. (**136**)

Du sang aussi pauvre que les menstrues d'une vieille fille sèche. (**138**)

[I]mpoli comme le fondement d'une chienne pleine. (**177**)

Le seul possédant du rigide entre les jambes. (**195**)

Secondly, the forcefulness and violence of these words and phrases emphasise the drama of life as depicted by the novel. Daily life is violent and full of risks; vehement, aggressive vocabulary conveys the atmosphere of almost constant conflict within which the characters are obliged to function. Examples are the argument which breaks out at Koné Ibrahima's funeral—'«Assois tes fesses et ferme la bouche!»' (**15**)—the beggars' attack on Salimata, the dispute between Salimata and Mariam, the disagreement between the traditional chiefs and the village council on Fama's arrival in Togobala, and the fracas following the guard's refusal to let Fama cross the border. Life is nothing but strife and discord in the Côte des Ébènes. Finally, as with proverbs, the constant stream of expletives is a valid transposition of everyday speech, as in the mouth of the apprentice driver Sery, speaking of the unwelcome arrival of foreign nationals in his country:

> ... en moins d'une semaine, nos concessions étaient devenues aussi répugnantes que les yeux et les nez de leurs marmailles qu'ils ne mouchaient jamais, aussi puantes que les fesses de leurs rejetons qu'ils ne torchent jamais. (**88**)

The excess in Kourouma's style, combined with the oaths and expletives, is associated with a kind of hopelessness, an ultimate negativity in relation to the black man, what presidential propagandist Maclédio defines as 'l'«afro-pessimisme»' (*En attendant*, p. 153). This negativity finds its most violent expression in a transition from third-person narrative into, and back out of, the focalisation of Fama, who compares the disgraceful lack of storm drains in Abidjan to the political climate of post-independence Africa with great virulence. In spite of the lack of an opening 'Que', or alternatively a comma after 'pardonne', the final sentence shapes less like a declarative statement than the narrator's direct plea for conduct unbecoming in a mosque to be indulgently overlooked:

> Dès lors, le ciel, comme si on l'en avait empêché depuis des mois, se déchargea, déversa des torrents qui noyèrent les rues sans égouts. Sans égouts, parce que les Indépendances ici aussi ont trahi, elles n'ont pas creusé les égouts promis et elles ne le feront jamais; des lacs d'eau continueront de croupir comme toujours et les nègres colonisés ou indépendants y pataugeront tant qu'Allah ne décollera pas la damnation qui pousse aux fesses du nègre. Bâtard de fils de chien! Pardon! Allah le miséricordieux pardonne d'aussi malséantes injures échappées à Fama dans la mosquée! (**27**)

The chaotic style, enlivened by exclamatory oaths and punctuation marks, conveys the disorder of post-independence African society. Nothing happens in a rational fashion; everything is topsy-turvy; the norms of civilised society have been overturned; greed, injustice, poverty and corruption have taken over. A mad world, my masters, quite literally absurd and Ubuesque.

Chapter Five

Writing West Africa

Location

It is not indifferent to consider at the outset some of the means whereby are established the geographical and temporal locations of novels set in West Africa, taken in the widest sense, by some of the significant authors mentioned above (p. 4). The area can be taken to mean not just the countries of what old atlases used to call 'Guinea' (the former colonies and mandated territories of Portugal, Great Britain and France, plus long-independent Liberia, along the Gulf of Guinea and its various Coasts, stretching from Senegal to Cameroon), but continuing down to the equatorial area formerly colonised by France, Spain and Belgium, including landlocked countries with little or no territorial access to the seaboard. The text of *Monnè, outrages et défis* is an open invitation to do so: the prestige of the holy warrior ('Almamy') Samory Touré radiates out from his Manding lands to suffuse 'la Négritie' (p. 27), i.e. what is West Africa in a narrower acceptance. Yet in an extension of its mythical currency, the area will then be considered to be the black Africa that extends down the western side of the continent as far as the equator, constituting the fiefdom of de Gaulle, one of the five major world players during World War Two: 'chef des empires du sud (les Arabies, les Négrities et les mers australes)' (*Monnè*, p. 209). Undeterred by the aborted landing of the Free French at Dakar:

> Après les libations et les sacrifices, de Gaulle descendit aux extrémités des Négrities à Brazzaville, y rassembla les Nègres de toutes les tribus, dont ceux de Soba. (*ibid.*, pp. 209-10)

Hence no apology is offered for widening the West African zone; indeed, it would be tempting to include settings created by writers of the stature of an indigenous anglophone writer, the Nigerian Ken Saro-Wiwa,[1] as well as topical to refer to Giles Foden, whose *The Last King of Scotland* (1998) is a portrayal of the notorious Ugandan dictator Idi Amin.[2] The restricted compass of this study, however, dictates a restriction to francophone literary production.

Given the anti-establishment criticisms often voiced, and the fact that the novel, a non-indigenous genre, might be a challenging one for any local target audience, there was a risk of its being considered, by zealous thought police of either former colonial or newly independent regimes, to be more of an incendiary device than in countries of more stable political democracy. In other words, writing was a committed activity that could lead to trouble, if not for the author, then for the family members who had remained behind in a country from which he himself had sought prudent and timely exile. One who endured persecution leading to lost employment was the father of Cameroonian author Ferdinand Oyono, and if a scoreline of Cameroon 3:0 Côte d'Ivoire could cause the latter's President Gueï, in 2000, to detain Olivier Tébily and his fellow Elephants for two days because they had rolled over and died in a match in which bragging rights in the Gulf were so clearly at stake, then one could not be too careful with respect to the printed word. Directly critical fiction might also be a juvenile peccadillo that could hinder a future career in politics or diplomacy; it was to be abandoned by Oyono, and filtered with great care by the Congolese writer Henri Lopes.

The country of Guinea, its capital, and other place names and geographical features (Conakry, Kouroussa, Siguiri, Tindican, Dabola, the Fouta-Djallon mountains), feature, it would seem unproblematically, in Camara Laye's pre-independence *L'Enfant noir* (1953). And why should they not, in a novel concerned with the

---

[1] Affinities with Kourouma have been detected by Patrick Corcoran, ' "Child" soldiers in Ken Saro-Wiwa's *Sozaboy* and Ahmadou Kourouma's *Allah n'est pas obligé*', *Mots pluriels*, 22 (septembre 2002).

[2] A film version (dir. Kevin Macdonald), starring Forest Whitaker as Amin, James McAvoy as Garrigan (the Bob Astles adviser role) and Kerry Washington went on general release in January 2007.

patriarchal simplicity of the author's native roots, and written with an unresentful animus towards the French coloniser by a culturally assimilated student in whom there is at the same time a tolerant and ecumenical spirit reflecting the *négritude* (*supra*, p. 4) movement? Yet even this seemingly ideal figure of mediator was to incur the displeasure of Sékou Touré, president from 1958 onwards, and had to seek exile in Senegal for the rest of his life. Sembene Ousmane's *Les Bouts de bois de Dieu* (1960), in its account of the epic struggle to drive a railway east from Dakar to Bamako, dealt with a subject of such national and syndical pride that there was no particular problem in its being temporally and locationally specific.

Fama may be seen as a Bunyanesque Everyman figure in his journey through the slough of despond of imprisonment and the associated daily trials and tribulations of daily life under the *Indépendances*. In a similar way, authors have tended to make of the countries in which their protagonists live a kind of Every<u>land</u>. For Lopes, keen perhaps not to nip a developing diplomatic career in the bud, the country that groans under the tyranny of Bwakamabé Na Sakkadé (modelled on President Mobutu of the then republic of Zaire) is called only 'le Pays', situated somewhere around the parallel of the equator, but not necessarily even in Africa, though seemingly so. In Oyono's *Une vie de boy*, a traditional framing device tells of how the narrator Toundi, whose notebooks are now being published as a sacred duty, is found dying in Spanish (now Equatorial) Guinea, to which he has fled from over the border in southern Cameroon. *Le Vieux Nègre et la médaille*, also published in the same year (1956) predating independence, bears only the names of two fictional towns, Doum and Tinda; its status as a companion volume to the autobiographical account emerges only from the involvement of the same missionary, Father Vandermayer, so that its Cameroonian setting is established only by indirection, and with circumspection.

If less necessarily from a strategy of prudent self-protection, the Caucasian writer Patrick Grainville, in *Les Flamboyants* (Prix Goncourt, 1976), also fictionalises the location of his account of the megalomania of a central African dictator, Tokor Yali Yulmata, who is based on Jean-Bédel Bokassa. In the dazzling verbal pyrotechnics which assault our senses, giving an impression of the clash of regional and ethnic interests within a country whose borders are clearly arbitrary in every sense except one of political convenience, it appears to emerge (and not even an authority on Grainville dares to be categorical) that the name of what is usually known as 'le pays yali' is Yulmatie. As for Alain Mabanckou, in *Les Petits-Fils nègres de Vercingétorix*, a standard novelistic device involves a *cahier*, containing an account of the country's troubles, and written under immense pressure by Hortense Iloki, being spirited away by her daughter from the hut where the door is being broken down by the eponymous, sanguinary *sudiste* soldiers intent on her murder. The country bears the conflated *mot-propre-valise* of 'le Viétongo', so there are no prizes for guessing that there is a north-south divide, and although the names of administrative capital 'Mapapouville' (Brazzaville) and commercial hub 'Pointe-Rouge' (Pointe-Noire) are to a degree tweaked, the liminary encyclopedic indications of its population (2,600,000) and surface area (342,000 sq. km.) leave the reader in no doubt that the location is the former French Republic of the Congo.

Samba Diallo, the protagonist of Cheikh Hamidou Kane's *L'Aventure ambiguë*, lives in a village whose cryptic name, 'L...', takes us back to the classical distancing device of, *inter alia*, a short novel to whose protagonist he bears some resemblance, Constant's *Adolphe*. J.P. Little contends, however, that the effect here is not so much neutralising as mythologising.[3] The unprepossessing little town of 'L...' is situated in 'le Pays des Diallobé', the suffixing itself an indication of the importance and rootedness of Samba's family in the area (cf. the inhabitants of Burkina-Faso, the Burkinabé). It has been established by the Littles' fieldwork that the fictional name is a transposition of the historic Tokolor province of Yirlabé, straddling the Senegal River, i.e. extending into Mauritania. When he goes to Paris to further his education, Samba Diallo meets fellow-countryman Pierre-Louis, retired international lawyer, who knew two of the first *députés* to come from the 'Pays des Diallobé' after World War Two, who by inference must have been Senegalese.

---

[3] J.P. Little, *Cheikh Hamidou Kane: 'L'Aventure ambiguë'* (London: Grant and Cutler, 2000), p. 13.

Yambo Ouologuem's *Le Devoir de violence* is as bitterly critical a novel as Kourouma's. However, it deals with a potentially unpalatable subject—that is was native Africans themselves, not the colonial powers, who first instituted slavery—stretching far further backwards into the historical time of the Mali empire, as far as the year 1202. One or two identifiable place names (Mostaganem; Algiers; Benghazi) occur in the history of the legendary dynasty of the Saïfs, of the equally fictitious Nakem empire, which would appear to be situated in Mali (formerly French Sudan) as it exists today. Chronologically, the major part of the narrative runs from the reign of an El Héit successor at the beginning of the twentieth century, a time period dealt with by Kourouma in the later *Monnè*, and it reaches no further than the end of World War Two.

In *Les Soleils des Indépendances*, it is a long time before there is any even perfunctory attempt to establish some serviceable referentiality concerning the novel's setting, except with respect to the mythical Worodougou homeland. Almost comic bewilderment is felt by Fama when he is confronted with arbitrary national frontiers that, to him, his own people's lands overarch: 'Fama étranger sur cette terre de Horodougou!' (**101**). He regards the river separating adjacent countries—the Gouaba, an affluent of the Gbanbala, the Sankarani and the Niger—as an irrelevancy in an undefined territory stretching west-north-west into Guinea, and doubtless even north through the Denguélé region towards Mali, from where his ancestors came. As for showing a national identity card (though he knows it makes sense since the *Indépendances*—**25**), the first time he blusteringly gets by without one (**101**), and on the second occasion, border tensions and restrictions on the movement of a released political detainee (**189**) would have negated even the (unlikely) production of one, and consequently precipitate his suicidal crossing. After 9/11, one could imagine the fuss if he attempted to fly to Mali without documents.

'La capitale' (**9**) of the country is just that, with not even a fictitious name being allocated, but its situation in proximity to a reddish-brown 'lagune […] latérite' (**12**; **20**) and its throbbing commercial vitality mean that it is certainly not Houphouët-Boigny's hubristic development of his Baoulé hometown, Yamoussoukro, with its immense basilica, the in retrospect ironically named Notre-Dame de la Paix. Eventually there are references to 'la République' (**95**, twice), and, invoking the polarity of ebony and ivory in a ludic and fairly transparent way, four to 'la République des Ébènes' (**156; 159; 175; 191**) and five, more unambiguously still, to 'la Côte des Ébènes' (**86; 87; 101; 154; 166**).[4]

This habit of cautious transposition does not desert Kourouma for a long time. In the political fable *En attendant le vote des bêtes sauvages* (1998), 'la République des Ébènes' and the major focus, 'la colonie du Golfe' (Togo) are thus designated throughout, with their presidents (and other dictators, such as Mobutu and Bokassa) being known by fictitious names, but nonetheless in terms of their well-known family totems—in the case of Houphouët-Boigny and Eyadema, 'l'homme au totem caïman' and 'l'homme au totem faucon', respectively. But in addition there is provided the following list, perhaps just to heighten the playfulness and confusion, of 'maints pays africains: la Côte-de-l'Or, la Côte d'Ivoire, le Nigeria, le Togo, le Dahomey et [...] la colonie du Golfe' (*En attendant*, p. 85), a confusion later dispelled, as we have seen in Mabanckou (*supra*, p. 60), by telltale encyclopedic details that square with the Togo entry: 'dans un pays de cinquante-six mille kilomètres carrés et de moins de quatre millions d'habitants' (*ibid.*, p. 302). In *Allah n'est pas obligé*, however, the picaresque soldier's tale of a naïve African Candide whose adventures begin over the border in Togobala and only end on the road to the capital of Côte d'Ivoire, actual designations of countries and capitals (*supra*, p. 10) are given from the outset—'au nord de la Côte d'Ivoire, en Guinée, et en d'autres républiques bananières et foutues comme Gambie, Sierra Leone, et Sénégal là-bas, etc.' (*Allah*, p. 10)—, there are postwar economic indicators, such as 'francs CFA', then actual dates. The emphasis will fall firmly on Côte d'Ivoire, its history and ethnic troubles, only in *Quand on refuse on dit non*, as Birahima listens with rapt attention to the lessons of the imam's beautiful daughter (see *supra*, p. 11).

---

[4] Conflating these names, and confusing them with the ghastly French euphemism that used to designate cargoes of slaves, Mortimer (p. 110) calls the republic the 'Bois d'Ébènes'.

The physical and allegorical environment

The sun of the title can refer to a period of time, and even to the street lights that burn all night in the capital (**100**), but it is equally a form of energy equal to the evils of the time, forceful enough to counter the malfeasance of government. Thus, the forces of nature, the blood of sacrifice, the wind and the sun are forever present and, therefore, more capable than its human victims of combating, or at least outlasting, the suns, i.e. *époques*, of independence. The sun also rises in a physical sense, influencing the lives of the characters and regulating their activities. Traditional ceremonies, such as female excision, take place according to the season: 'un matin de la dernière semaine de l'harmattan' (**35**). The use of the plural noun indicates the passing of periods of time, as in the chapter title 'Les soleils sonnant l'harmattan' (**120**), where the word 'soleils' means days. The epithets associated with the sun conjur up an entity of unimaginable power, similar to Allah, whose workings are incomprehensible to human beings. Phrases such as 'Au large, seul maître et omniprésent, le soleil' (**51**) remind the European reader of how the elements, most particularly the sun, dominate life in an African country, making it impossible to carry on daily life at certain times of the day or in certain seasons. The sun permeates this novel to such an extent that it could be said to be a character. Other natural elements are personified, e.g. the fog in the following sentence: 'Le brouillard de l'harmattan se crut un chef de l'ancien temps et s'appropria montagnes, routes et brousse' (**100**). It is the sun, though, that is omnipotent, taking precedence over all other natural phenomena.

The coastal region, where the capital is situated, has a sticky, humid climate, whereas Fama's home region is an arid land of savannah. He hates the storms—'Bâtardes! déroutantes, dégoûtantes, les entre-saisons de ce pays mélangeant soleils et pluies' (**12**)—and the way he has lost touch with his roots during 'ses vingt ans de sottises dans la capitale' (**96**), and loves the climate of his childhood, with the buffeting harmattan wind, nostalgically attached to the dry harshness of the landscape, with its flame-trees (**94**), the giant silk-cotton tree of Togobala that can be seen from afar (**102**), and 'le baobab du marché' (**103**). The light reflected on the sea creates a beautiful backdrop for the city, an oasis of tranquillity in the turbulent mêlée of urban life. The sun is symbolic of life itself, as in the following comparison with Fama's present existence: 'Cette vie-là n'était-elle pas un soleil éteint et assombri dans le haut de sa course?' (**31**; *supra*, p. 1). The lyrical sentences which evoke the sun and its light in this novel are associated with beauty and with a positive, life-giving force: 'Et le matin d'harmattan comme toute mère commençait d'accoucher très péniblement l'énorme soleil d'harmattan' (**121**). This sentence opens a passage where the sun is personified; the literary device serves to emphasise the fact that the sun and the wind are closely associated, in the rural areas, with the world of the spirits and that of traditional beliefs and stories. These paragraphs lead on to Balla's playing of the grumpy old man in his disparagement of the wimpish current season in comparison with 'les vrais harmattans' (**122**) of the past, and seamlessly prompt the embedded story of Balla's epic encounter and contract with the genie of the hunt. During Fama's imprisonment, the light of the sun seems to be extinguished and he knows only a deathly darkness, expressed by the chiasmus of: 'Ce camp était la nuit et la mort, la mort et la nuit' (**160**).

On another level, the natural world is an integral part of the language and metaphor of Kourouma's style, since comparisons between man and the rich local bestiary are made constantly, and African proverbs are invoked as comments on characters or events. Local colour can occasionally be painted, in an amusing backwards direction, on to Europe, as when Hitler's underground bunker in Berlin—'les boyaux de pangolin de son palais' (*Monnè*, p. 210)—is likened to an anteater's burrow. *Les Soleils des Indépendances* features an unusual system of metaphors. On the one hand, they compare humans and events to animals and natural elements: 'un homme nu comme un tronc de baobab' (**164**); 'toute la caserne vibrait, bruissait du brouhaha de l'orage battant la forêt' (**172**). On the other, the reversal of this procedure, pathetic fallacy, takes place when natural scenes are likened to human laments, as in the following sentence: 'De là le quartier nègre, le pont, la lagune entière s'ouvraient et s'étendaient jusqu'à l'infini comme des chansons d'excisées' (**51**). The reference to the excision ceremony is in keeping with Salimata's train of thought, as her everyday activities of cooking and selling the spiced rice with which she makes a living for herself and Fama are interrupted by the horrific memories of her genital mutilation and rape. This device whereby, unusually, the natural world is compared to the human one, shows that the perspective of the narration has shifted to Salimata's point of view. Through this metaphor, the author veers away from omniscient third-person narration and reverts to the stream of consciousness, giving the reader information about Salimata's state of mind. Even the beauty of the natural scene is perceived in terms of her memory of the excision ceremony.

In an interview with Jean Ouédraogo, Kourouma comments on his use of what he calls African 'cosmology' by explaining that, when he was growing up there was a close relationship between wild animals and the inhabitants of towns and villages. He wishes to convey the importance of the animal world to the lives of the African community:

> Rien ne se faisait sans que les animaux ne soient mêlés: les proverbes, les façons de faire. (Ouédraogo, p. 777)

Authorial intention goes further, however, than a simple wish to convey the 'exotic' nature of African society to a Western reader. Kourouma's intention is to preserve and maintain African history and cosmology. He sees the world as being out of balance, in that African readers are bombarded with the culture of the West and know little about their own culture. Kourouma's fictional work provides an account of African history and uses as its tools the myths, proverbs, language and imagery of Africa.

The concept of the totem is central to the use of images in *Les Soleils des Indépendances*. The animist belief that each object has its own genie, or *kala*, which leads to a respect for the forces of nature and an inherent desire to protect or renew the environment is reflected in the images of the novel. As portrayed by Balla in the novel (**119**), the *dja* or double of the person is their counterpart in the spirit world; the *dja* could be present in any object or animal, hence it is prudent to treat all animals or natural objects with respect. Yet one clings above all to one's family totem; Fama bridles when his family is linked with the Keitas, and the narrator intervenes to say why:

> Qui n'est pas Malinké peut l'ignorer; en la circonstance, c'était un affront à faire éclater les pupilles. Qui donc avait associé Doumbouya et Keita? Ceux-ci sont rois du Ouassoulou et ont pour totem l'hippopotame et non la panthère. (**13**)[5]

That Fama should be ripped by the jaws of a cayman crocodile is a neat touch that does well to remain implicit in the text, unless 'les gros caïmans sacrés' (**191**) is tantamount to saying it. For everybody knew that the cayman was the family totem of Félix Houphouët-Boigny, who had a marble-lined *plan d'eau* built for his favourite reptiles (*En attendant*, pp. 187-8), so that a precise embodiment of 'la bâtardise', as it were, actually kills the protagonist.

In Laye's *L'Enfant noir* (ch. III) the boy's uncle demonstrates knowledge both of folk tales in the European tradition (Aesop's 'The Tortoise and the Hare', via La Fontaine) and indigenous African ones, such as how the panther was tricked by the monkey, and how the palm-squirrel held out on the hyena the whole night long. In Mabanckou's *Les Petits-Fils de Vercingétorix*, Christiane is immensely impressed to hear her Congolese boyfriend Gaston (an 'assimilated' forename), who is a humble port employee, recite the treasured francophone educational soundbite of La Fontaine's 'Le Chêne et le Roseau', while schoolteacher Kimbembé conscientiously reads to daughter Maribé the fables of Florian and of La Fontaine.

Kourouma too works the *topoi* of fables into his text, comparing his characters' behaviour to animal ways throughout the text and employing proverbs to reinforce the commentary on human action. A series of links between the human and animal world is created, for instance 'l'hyène a beau être édentée, sa bouche ne sera jamais un lieu de passage pour le cabrin' (**17**). The beast is soon back, in 'où a-t-on vu l'hyène déserter les environs des cimetières et le vautour l'arrière des cases?' (**19**). These relationships between human and

---

[5] In fact, though, he is later said to have 'une cousine mariée à un Keita' (**110**).

animal extend, then, into the world of the spirit; whilst testing the credulity of the reader and proposing a sceptical authorial standpoint, Kourouma nonetheless demonstrates the validity of the belief in magic for the communities portrayed in the novel. Taking one situation as an example, that of the conflict which results from Fama's polygamy on bringing Mariam into his household, the animal comparisons are vivid and colourful:

> Mariam gênait et elle était moqueuse comme une mouche et, disait-on, féconde comme une souris.
>
> Les deux co-épouses comme deux poules s'assaillirent […].
>
> … on ne ressemble pas des oiseaux quand on craint le bruit des ailes. Et les soucis qui chauffaient Fama avaient été bien mérités; ils étaient l'essaim de mouches qui forcément harcèle celui qui a réuni un troupeau de crapauds. (**152-3**)

There is a visual appeal in these comparisons, and the movement evoked by chickens fighting and flies buzzing brings the incidents to life. The animal images play a significant role in evoking the intense vitality of the African urban scene, but their significance goes much further than this stylistic device, because these images depict and reinforce the portrayal of the energy which, when the belief in magic holds sway, mutate from human to animal to spirit world: 'Des genies, des mânes, des aïeux, et même des animaux avaient profité de ce rassemblement et s'étaient ajoutés à la foule' (**145**).

Animals also feature in dreams and portents, and it is no surprise that Fama's nightmare—'Ah! ce rêve qui fumait la mort et la peur!' (**163**)—involves a termitarium and a ferocious, human-sodomising baboon. Perhaps it should have been laid before the competent soothsayers (called elsewhere, with impeccable, though no doubt tongue-in-cheek exactness of derivation, 'les onirocritiques'—*Monné*, p. 94), but Fama seems to have worked out this complex allegory for himself. His friend Bakary urges him not to bother, thinking that the French-trained civil servants who now rule the roost in the *Indépendances* will not be interested in such mumbo-jumbo: 'Ces jeunes gens débarqués de l'au-delà des mers ne pensent plus comme des nègres' (**165**). Perhaps; but the all-seeing 'dictateur au totem caïman' (*En attendant*, p. 185 *et passim*), who always remains within the information loop, no such pieces of apparently irrelevant data are indifferent. More to the point than the significance of the dream for Nakou is the fact that when the mysterious woman in white indicates the successive doors that must be gone through to find not a home, but a 'qualité d'homme' (**164**)—i.e. the way to one's true self?—, she concludes her message with the following cryptic words: '«[R]appelle-toi qu'un malheur, quel que soit l'homme atteint, ne nous est jamais étranger, jamais lointain, bien au contraire… bien au contraire… bien au contraire»' (*ibid.*). Need one say more?

Kourouma's employment of comparisons from the natural world is one way in which he alerts the reader to the presence in Africa of a world beyond the material; Gassama refers to 'ses tentatives de faire éclater les frontières du monde visible pour le charger des valeurs de l'ontologie négro-africaine' (p. 86). Through the striking nature of the imagery, the reader is made aware of the symbiosis between the human and the natural world in the African context.

Narrative

Narrative and narration have already been mentioned on several occasions,[6] and will now be considered more fully. Kourouma is a superior literary craftsman and, in terms of narratorial competence, delivers all the satisfactions one is entitled to expect. Examples have been given of standard shifts from interior monologue in *style indirect libre* (free indirect style) to third-person omniscience, and here is one of *style direct libre*. It moves out of a subjective and self-motivational take, or focalisation, on events that would not be beyond the protagonist's cultural and educational competence, via the linking and catapulting effect of what is known as the '*et* de mouvement', into third-person narrative that reflects a more neutral and studied (e.g. 'faire l'exégèse des dires') voice:

---

[6] *Supra*, pp. 20; 38; 46; 51; 56; 65.

> Réfléchis à des choses sérieuses, légitime descendant des Doumbouya! Es-tu, oui ou non, le dernier, le dernier descendant de Souleymane Doumbouya? Ces soleils sur les têtes, ces politiciens, tous ces voleurs et menteurs, tous ces déhontés, ne sont-ils pas le désert bâtatd où doit mourir le fleuve Doumbouya? Et Fama commença de penser à l'histoire de la dynastie, pour interpréter les choses, faire l'exégèse des dires afin de trouver sa propre destinée. **(96-97)**

There is a lively and amusing shift from direct- to reported-speech simulation (i.e. *style indirect libre*) in Diakité's bombardment of Fama with questions as he settles down to the journey in Ouedrago's truck: '«Que la paix soit avec toi, Fama!» dit-il avant de poursuivre. Depuis combien de saisons Fama n'était-il pas parti au pays? Des années? Depuis des années? Dans ce cas, de nombreuses et désagréables surprises l'attendaient là-bas' **(83)**.

In keeping with the remit of this chapter, to highlight the cultural specificity of Kourouma's text, a realistic aim would be to restrict consideration to aspects of narrative pertinent to the function of a specific stance vis-à-vis the narratees of this story, and ones which define an unusual, personalised narratorial identity.

a) Storytelling

'Mais asseyons-nous, et restons autour du n'goni des chasseurs' **(143)** is the kind of invitation that would have been obeyed by Kourouma as a boy, and a polite imperative to which the Queen and the Duke of Edinburgh must have had no choice but to submit on many an occasion. A dance forms an interlude to a story being told.

The narrative style in *Les Soleils des Indépendances* reflects this West African tradition, and the Islamic preference for recital, referred to above (pp. 25-26). Portents, dreams and the supernatural bulk large, and are relayed at face value, as articles of common belief. A feeling of *orature*, as much, if not more, than *écriture* is also engendered by the attitude of the narrator towards his audience. The phatic, gestural aspect of storytelling, in which interaction takes place and the raconteur must think on his feet in reacting to dubiety or hostility, is revealed at the beginning of the third paragraph, after the account of the journey back home of Koné Ibrahima's shade:

> Vous paraissez sceptique! Eh bien, moi, je vous le jure, et j'ajoute: si le défunt était de caste forgeron, si l'on n'était pas dans l'ère des Indépendances (les soleils des Indépendances, disent les Malinkés), je vous le jure, on n'aurait jamais osé l'inhumer dans une terre lointaine et étrangère. (**9-10**)

Such a pose recalls that of the Stendhalian narrator of *Le Rouge et le Noir*, in whom the first-person *je* breaks cover at times, covering his tracks before an unconvinced audience when telling of how Julien Sorel thought that 'il serait utile à son hypocrisie d'aller faire une station à l'église. Ce mot vous surprend?' (I, 5), or castigating the listeners' own hypocrisy when explaining that a novel is a mirror held up by the narrator to society: 'Et l'homme qui porte ce miroir dans sa hotte sera par vous accusé d'être immoral!' (II, 18). A further example of this interplay with an imagined audience is the call to share the astonishment of the narrator when the last prince of the Doumbouyas is asked to produce something so trivial as an identity card: 'Avez-vous bien entendu? Fama étranger sur cette terre de Horodougou!' (**101**).

Rosemary Schikora says of this narrative effect: 'We are perhaps as close here as possible in a written text to simulating a participatory audience a crucial component of traditional oral performance' (p. 814). The *mise en scène* achieved, one which begets more storytellers in the way that a Malinké funeral is the pretext for more stories, is reminiscent of Homi Bhabha's distinction between the pedagogic and the performative as articulated with reference to 'the people [of the nation] as an *a priori* historical presence, a pedagogical object; and the people constructed in the performance of narrative' (pp. 298-9). The vitality and pace of Kourouma's novel, as well as the impression of events occurring before one's eyes in the narrative present of the storyteller's address, seem to portray the characteristics of Bhabha's concept of performance, an opportunity 'ultimately [to] involve the whole laborious telling of the collectivity itself' (p. 292, quoting Fredric Jameson).

It is not enough, though, to imagine a close-knit audience of local, soon to be empowered listeners witnessing a heterodiegetic *conteur* holding forth in the style of Birago Diop's Amadou Koumba. For if whether a single person or more is being addressed is indeterminable when cultural information is supplied to a non-Malinké addressee by means of an amusingly hyperbolic sentence such as 'Qui n'est pas Malinké peut l'ignorer: en la circonstance c'était un affront à faire éclater les pupilles' (**13**), the same does not apply to 'Mais le sang, vous ne le savez pas parce que vous qui n'êtes pas Malinké' (**141**). Here, only the lower-case adjective would be invariable (for Kourouma, anyway), and if a more unambiguous example is sought, there is no need to look further than 'Vous paraissez sceptique!' (**9**). Considering that even deferential address takes place in the familiar *tu* form, as when the respectable, older Fama is greeted by some young men (**83**), spoken to in a dream (**164**) or gently bidden to be calm by a paramedic (**194**), then it follows that a single interlocutor from beyond the simulated situation of storytelling, indeed maybe not belonging to the Malinké ethnicity, is the narratee who is being appealed to in such instances. The conclusion would appear to be that Kourouma is engaging, as well as with the listener to a tale, with the reader of a book sitting in the developed francophone world, whose unknown quantity is underlined by the *vous* form of address. Hence the storytelling aspect so often referred to with respect to *Les Soleils des Indépendances* has an additional dimension and edge to it.

The yarn seems to be spun in a leisurely fashion, but occasional reminders of the need to take short cuts draw attention to the performative act. Cousin Lacina's preferment, because humiliating to Fama, may be quickly glossed over: 'Parlons-en rapidement plutôt. [...] Savez-vous ce qui advint?' (**23**), but on the other hand, the telling of a particularly juicy anecdote, the daring exploit of Balla hunting the black buffalo, should be delayed no longer, although then not rushed: 'Un exemple: l'exploit triomphal lors des funérailles du père de Fama. Empressons-nous de le conter' (**123**).

Give or take forty-two lines after the short introductory paragraph of the novel, and allowing for the different tenses which smooth out the admittedly strange sequence adopted in the earlier of them, it ends as it has begun, with a Malinké having died and a forty-day mourning period beginning:

> Il y avait une semaine qu'avait fini dans la capitale Koné Ibrahima, de race malinké [...].
> Des jours suivirent le jour des obsèques jusqu'au septième jour et les funérailles du septième jour se déroulèrent devant l'ombre, puis se succédèrent des semaines et arriva le quarantième jour et les funérailles du quarantième jour ont été fêtées [...]. **(9-10)**

> Un Malinké était mort. Suivront les jours jusqu'au septième jour et les funérailles du septième jour, puis se succéderont les semaines et arrivera le quarantième jour et frapperont les funérailles du quarantième jour et... **(196)**

Comforting circularity rather than depressing linearity is thereby stressed. This structural rhetorical device, characteristic of the *rondeau* poem (cf. Voiture's 'À vous ouïr, Chapelain [...] À vous ouïr.'), gives a gratifying sense of closure and completeness to the reading or listening audience, and seems recuperable both to the art of storytelling and to animist beliefs.[7] It is known in French (though definitions and terminology in this area are not common to all critics) as 'inclusion'.[8] It could be argued that another *Canterbury Tales* effect is created here, in that Koné Ibrahima's death begets the tale of one of his mourners, Fama, whereupon Fama's death could spark off another narrative, and so on. The three suspension points leave matters as unconcluded as the existence of mankind, in general if not in particular, and suggest a 'moulin à contes' effect of tales only waiting to be told.

Chapter headings, as they operate in *Les Soleils des Indépendances* and *Monnè, outrages et défis*, operate as a further storytelling device, giving the audience an idea of what is upcoming. As such, they are much more striking examples of the invitation to order and sequence that is extended to the reader by one of Roland Barthes's five narrative

---

[7] A good comparator is Koyaga's hunting exploits (*En attendant*, pp. 70; 71; 73; 75) and killing of rivals for dictatorial power (pp. 100-1; 116-7; 119), when tails and penises are stuffed into the mouths of the dead so that evil spirits (*nyamas*) are not let out. Here, no confusing ambiguity is allowed to hover.

[8] B. Dupriez, *Gradus: les procédés littéraires* (Union Générale d'Éditions, «10/18» [1984]), pp. 251-2.

codes, the proairetic, than any that he, or Jean Duffy, in her explanatory gloss of what he meant, provide.⁹ These 'Wherein...', 'In which...', 'Containing...' and '*Comment...*' summaries of content and plot can be traced back at least as far as the picaresque adventures related in Fielding's *Tom Jones* and Voltaire's *Candide*. Further textbook examples reflecting a storytelling situation, this time in the French Caribbean, may be found in the Prix Goncourt-winning novel *Texaco*, by Patrick Chamoiseau.¹⁰

Schikora (p. 815) is broadly correct, but a touch too sweeping, in saying that: 'Each of the eleven chapter titles closely resembles a folk saying in the oblique, economical phrasing of proverbial language'. The anything but tautological 'Les choses qui ne peuvent pas être dites ne méritent pas de noms' (III, 1) has been dealt with above (pp. 52-53). I, 1, 'Le molosse et sa déhontée façon de s'asseoir', on the dumb Doberman that always flaunts its balls as it sits down,¹¹ anticipates the chapter's final, proverbial sentence, about Fama's short fuse. These 'trailers' can create scary suspense, as in II, 3: 'Les meutes de margouillats et de vautours trouèrent ses côtes; il survécut grâce au savant Balla' (**105**), but the deadly physical danger turns out to be no more, though maybe this is more than enough, than nightmarish oneiric content (**119**). II, 1: 'Mis à l'attache par le sexe, la mort s'approchait et gagnait; heureusement la lune perça et le sauva' (**81**), announces how Diakité will be humiliatingly tied up by his manhood to the pillar of a bridge, only to make his escape, guided by the moon, after his father has gone on the rampage and shot up the local party hierarchy. (No finer example of an ambiguous, 'hanging' participle could be found than 'Mis'.) I, 3: 'Le cou chargé de carcans hérissés de sortilèges comme le sont de piquants acérés les colliers

---

⁹ See Barthes, *S/Z* (Paris: Seuil, coll. 'Points', 1970), pp. 26-27. Duffy (*Structuralism: Theory and Practice* [Glasgow University French and German Publications, 1992], p. 65), drawing her examples from Roger Martin du Gard's *Jean Barois*, writes: 'The proairetic code relates to the process by which the reader synthesizes or "blocks out" data into sequences, which can then be given a name.'

¹⁰ For instance, 'ANNONCIATION (où l'urbaniste qui vient pour raser l'insalubre quartier Texaco tombe dans un cirque créole et affronte la parole d'une femme-matador)'; 'AUTOUR DE SAINT-PIERRE (où l'esclave Esternome lancé à la conquête de l'En-ville n'en ramène que l'horreur d'une [*sic*] amour grillée)', etc.

¹¹ Cf. La Fontaine, *Fables*, VIII, 16, 'L'Horoscope': 'Rien ne change un tempérament'.

du chien chasseur de cynocéphales' (**32**), is basically a mug-shot of a wanted rapist, Tiécoura, who is then described thus, less the spiked collar (**40**). Concrete and abstract clash, at least to Western ears, in 'hérissés de sortilèges'. The delicately poetic II, 2: 'Marcher à pas comptés dans la nuit du cœur et dans l'ombre des yeux' (**92**) turns out to be two verses of a wistful wedding song dealing with struggle in a world rendered hostile after the death of one's parents (**102**; see also **184**, for the one that Salimata is remembered as cheerfully singing as she pounds her meal).

Yet the most curious chapter heading, containing layers of exoticism and Malinké grammatical shortcuts with which a reader of a non-West African culture will struggle, is II, 4: 'Les soleils sonnant l'harmattan et Fama, avec les nuits hérissées de punaises et de Mariam, furent tous pris au piège; mais la bâtardise ne gagna pas' (**120**). Hardly clipped and 'economical', *pace* Schikora, this 'salmigondis' (as Kourouma will elsewhere describe dog's breakfasts of ideological slogans—*Monnè*, p. 278) is a baggy résumé of chapter content. The suns rise to announce the harmattan season, then there is zeugma (see *supra*, p. 50), in that Fama's nights (in an idiosyncratic acceptance of the verb 'hérisser')[12] are plagued by *thoughts* of the widow as well as the less tender ministrations of the bugs and kindred roaches. Fama and Mariam, it seems implied, are *both* (in an apparent ellipsis of 'tous deux') caught in a honey-pot sex trap, for the expression 'prendre au piège' refers to a spell Balla has promised to cast, which threatens disastrous consequences for the reproductive organ of any villager other than Fama who attempts the merry widow's virtue.

All of which is passing strange, but stranger still is the contention that bastardy does not prevail in the land. In order to assert his chieftain's rights, and bearing in mind his colourful past record as a counter-revolutionary dissident (**56-57**), Fama must bow the knee, brush the ground with his lips, and swear on the Qur'an his allegiance to the dictates of the party, the local committee president,

---

[12] There is a challenging pronominal use (**44**), and the chapter heading contains ellipsis of the previously expressed 'Le lit de bambou était hérissé de mandibules, était grouillant de punaises et de poux' (**96**).

and the revolution. This is intolerable to his pride, and president Babou is evidently worried about the uncompromising diktat handed down from national level: culturally, this will simply not play in Peoria. Hence, after a meeting with the village elders at dead of night—'Malheur à celui qui laissera transpirer un bout!' warns the narrator, himself significantly drawn into the conspiratorial proceedings (**136**)—, a face-saving fudge is worked out. The next day both sides get down on their knees and plead with the 'délégué étranger', from party HQ, to back off and accept Fama's application to become a card-carrying member of the socialist party. Dumbfounded, 'joué' as was intended (*ibid.*), he agrees to let things be. Yet quite how this is turned into a moral defeat for the 'bâtardise', of the post-independence period is hard to fathom. Certainly it has required not inconsiderable mental gymnastics and contortions, i.e. a lavish application of political 'spin', and it is to this aspect of the narrative that we now turn.

b) Spin doctoring

The word 'epic' has so far been taken as read,[13] as were narration and narrative earlier, yet once it is more exactly defined its relevance to *Les Soleils des Indépendances* will become clear. According to a reliable glossary definition, the term 'epic' refers to 'a long narrative poem on a serious subject, told in a formal and elevated style, and centred on a heroic or quasi-divine figure on whose actions depend the fate of a tribe, a nation, or […] the human race'.[14] This seems largely applicable to the story of the destiny of Fama Doumbouya. The epic poem is 'a ceremonial performance, and is narrated in a ceremonial style' (p. 55), and, extracting the term from the generic definition of poem: 'The term "epic" is often applied, by extension, to narratives which differ in many respects from this model but manifest the epic spirit and grandeur of the scale, the scope, and the

---

[13] See *supra*, pp. 7; 29; 49.

[14] M.H. Abrams, *A Glossary of Literary Terms* (Fort Worth, TX: Harcourt Brace Jovanovich, 6th ed., 1981), pp. 53-55 [p. 53].

profound human importance of their subjects' (p. 55). Further to provide theoretical underpinning to this mode:

> Since the writings of Plato and Aristotle [...] there has been an enduring division of the overall literary domain into three large generic classes, in terms of who speaks in the work: *lyric* (uttered throughout in the first person); *epic* or *narrative* (in which the narrator speaks in the first person, then lets his characters speak for themselves); and *drama* (in which the characters do all the talking). (p. 76)

Mutatis mutandis, such a definition could not be more applicable to this novel. Granted, the narration is mainly third-person, but a spokesman for the interests of the family line emerged on the first page ('Vous paraissez sceptique! Eh bien, moi...'—**9**), and beyond this occasional '*je*', a royal 'we', i.e. the first-person *plural*, comes frequently to the fore, praising the Malinkés and one of their more noble members. Step forward the griot, often mentioned earlier but now considered in his involvement with the style in which the novel is written, representing as he does 'a traditional protagonist whose contact with European culture is minimal' (Mortimer, p. 119).

If the best transliteration of what a *féticheur* does and stands for is 'witch doctor', then no doubt the most serviceable one for the griot is 'spin doctor'. When the trouble the French have with finding a satisfactory translation of this expression is recalled,[15] then the word 'griot', quite well known and of venerable pedigree, seems a very attractive proposition. We are reminded of Turoldus, allegedly the scribe of *La Chanson de Roland*, and whose epic poem (*chanson de geste*) is permeated by the unshakable belief that, in this holy war, 'Paien unt tort et chrestïens unt dreit' (l. 1015). Ouologuem (*Le Devoir de violence*, p. 10), preludes an account of a massacre with: 'le griot Koutouli, de précieuse mémoire, achève ainsi sa geste'. A more vulgar, but significant, comparator might be Assurancetourix, the harp-bearing bard of the Gauls. And finally, the poetic instance of the south-facing stone steles of Victor Segalen, is that of imperial

---

[15] 'Chargé des relations publiques d'un parti politique' (*Harrap's Shorter*) or 'consultant en communication attaché à un parti politique' (*O.U.P. Hachette*) seem ponderous explanatory glosses, though 'chargé d'image' is neatly inventive.

dynastic propagandist: 'Vous! fils de Han [...,] gardez-vous de cette méprise', as the Chinese addressees are apostrophised in 'Aux dix mille années'. What then is so strange about the narrator's here playing a similar role, that (albeit with less mediatic devices) of spin doctor Maclédio to Koyaga (in *En attendant*)?

In *Monnè, outrages et défis*, the griot praise-singer is defined thus:

> Les griots sont les frères de sang des nobles. Ce sont d'authentiques nobles dont les aïeux, à l'époque préislamique du Mandingue, ont accepté la déchéance pour louanger. Un noble ne paraissait pas sans être accompagné de son panégyriste. (p. 41)

The nobleman does not normally deign to speak, leaving this to his griot: why have a dog and bark, especially when this particular dog knows infinitely more about the family history? He is not necessarily a kinsman, e.g. in *Monnè*, in which the famous Djéliba wants to give up 'la grioterie' and put his harp away, but is coerced into serving King Djigui (*ibid.*, pp. 43-44). In *En attendant le vote des bêtes sauvages*, Bingo is player of the cora harp and 'le griot musicien de la confrérie des chasseurs' (p. 9). He delivers the *donsomana*, or purifying account of his master Koyaga's life, in the traditional way, with comic relief being provided by his 'répondeur' Tiécoura, who plays the flute, cracks obscene jokes, performs vulgar stage business, and has the jester's licence to hurl insults at the dictator without giving offence.

The role of the griot (the African equivalent of the Irish *seanachai*) at the funeral is as master of ceremonies who announces the participants as they arrive, giving an account of their family history and their relationship to the deceased. In the first chapter, Fama is insulted by Koné Ibrahima's griot, who (deliberately?) associates his family, the Doumbouya, with the Keitas, whose totem is the hippopotamus. Fama is not accompanied by 'Diamourou [...,] mon fidèle griot' (**107**), who remains in Togobala, and has to rise rather unconvincingly to the challenge himself. Diamourou even appears ['(évidemment avec les retouches et les explications du griot)'—**117**] to be willing to help out Balla, if Doumbouya family praises are to be sung, making the hunting anecdotes more than usually boring. But if no griot, any more than the traditional conjuring tricks at a funeral

(**143-4**), now measures up to historical precedent ('Plus de vrai griot: les réels sont morts avec les grands maîtres de guerre d'avant la conquête des Toubabs'—**14**), then the narrator is more than able to step in and bury the puny, sly stirrer, with his 'cris d'avocette' (**16**), who attempts to demean the Doumbouyas. The minutes of the meeting, as it were, will attempt to reinstate the last prince of the line in his prestige.

In many of the important interventions of the novel, the narrator expresses a griot viewpoint. It is important to note that this goes beyond the one underlying the historical narratives of *Monnè* and Ouologuem's *Le Devoir de violence*, in which the relation of what has happened, 'la geste', appears to devolve on the family historian and genealogist, i.e. the griot. Certainly in the first part of the latter novel it is said that there are two versions of a story, one of them the griots', some references to lineage and tradition, and many pious Islamic ejaculations, making it that Frederic Michelman will find greater validity in the argument that Kourouma is first to use the griot-narrator in a *sustained* manner.[16]

The previous chapter (*supra*, p. 56) ended with analysis of some impotent blasphemies uttered by Fama (**27**) that, it is hoped, all-seeing Allah will deign to excuse. Although they are well capable of reading between the lines, trusting to the tale rather than the teller, such a mitigating plea, uttered in an exclamatory tone, shortly to be followed by an rueful apostrophe to the central character— 'Blasphème! Gros péché! Fama, ne te voyais-tu pas en train de pécher dans la demeure d'Allah?' (**30**)—strikes Western readers accustomed to Flaubertian authorial impersonality as a little disconcerting. Nor, as narrator, is the spin doctor the slippery, unreliable figure so beloved of Western postmodern sophisticates, but rather a figure who is strong in his ideological commitment to the interests of the Doumbouya family: a Diamourou, if one likes, given a voice that is both exclamatory and impassioned. True, there is the occasional mischievous aside, such as the '(dommage que le

---

[16] Michelman, F., 'Independence and Disillusion in *Les Soleils des Indépendances*: A New Approach', in D.F. Dorsey, P.A. Ehegura and S.H. Arnold (eds.), *Design and Intent in African Literature* (Washington, DC: Three Continents, 1982), 91-95 (p. 95).

boubou ait été poussiéreux et froissé!)' that makes Fama's slinky progression more Pink Panther- than pantherlike (**103**), or the embarrassed reaction to his whoring (**56**), and a veil might have been drawn over some of the rival griot's more disrespectful remarks about the prince's 'four funerals and a wedding' existence (**18**), but epic discourse does not have to be of blinkered ideological commitment—'Qui aime bien châtie bien'—and overall, loyalty and pity are expressed for the dilemmas this ordinary man now finds himself in (cf. 'Ignorant que tu étais...'—**146**). In the following examples, first the griot bemoans Fama's fate, then, in *style indirect libre* (in which 'Lui, Fama' can be reread as 'Moi, Fama'), the sponger himself:

> Fama Doumbouya! Vrai Doumbouya, père Doumbouya, mère Doumbouya, dernier et légitime descendant des princes Doumbouya du Horodougou, totem panthère, était un «vautour». Un prince Doumbouya! Totem panthère faisait bande avec les hyènes. Ah! les soleils des Indépendances! (**11**)

> Lui, Fama, né dans l'or, le manger, l'honneur et les femmes! Éduqué pour préférer l'or à l'or, pour choisir le manger parmi d'autres, et coucher sa favorite parmi cent épouses! Qu'était-il devenu? Un charognard... (**12**)

Although sometimes appearing to address an audience of his master's kinsmen ('Dites-moi, en bon Malinké que pouvait-il chercher encore?'—**14**) the griot's task is also to put across Malinké views and norms (such as that it is manly to carry a knife, and O.K. to brandish it—**17**; **82**) to a readership unfamiliar with such ways: 'Tout cela dans le sang. Mais le sang, vous ne le savez pas parce que vous n'êtes pas Malinké, le sang est prodigieux, criard et enivrant' (**141**). As for the homeland that shimmers in the distance of pre-independence memory, which it has to be said is more by way of a mirage, the nostalgia is shared:

> Oh! Horodougou! tu manquais à cette ville et tout ce qui avait permis à Fama de vivre une enfance heureuse de prince manquait aussi (le soleil, l'honneur et l'or) [...]. Qui pouvait s'aviser alors d'apprendre à courir de sacrifice en sacrifice pour mendier? (**21**)

This passionate partisanship enlivens the presentation of Fama's inner debates, as here, where the present tenses, i.e. *style direct libre*, are mixed with warning, apostrophising, Macbethian predictions:

> Tu ne leur échapperas pas! tu ne pourras pas refuser l'héritage. Au village, les langues sont vraiment accrocheuses, mielleuses. Que faire alors? devrait-il renoncer au voyage? retourner dans la capitale? Non, ce n'est pas possible. Personne n'y songerait. C'est impossible. Dans ce cas, prépare-toi donc à hériter. (**90**)

And the narrator waxes apoplectic when the protagonist's naïve optimism, or spirit of humble resignation, risk being misunderstood:

> Maintenant, dites-le-moi! Le retour de Fama dans la capitale […], vraiment, dites-le-moi, cela était-il vraiment, vraiment nécessaire? Non et non! Or le voyage de Fama portait un sort très maléfique. (**146**)

> Était-ce dire que Fama allait à Togobala pour se refaire une vie? Non et non! Aussi paradoxal que cela puisse paraître, Fama partait dans le Horodougou pour y mourir le plus tôt possible. (**185**)

Scratch this type of personalised narrative posture, and you will find a Malinké underneath. One with all the 'fils d'esclave'-hating class bias of his master, a decent Muslim, and firmly anti-animist. Balla, whose come-uppance the reader has been promised (**105**), is portrayed with a degree of contempt, and his death elicits praise with loud damns:

> Ah! avant longtemps le Horodougou ne connaîtrait pas un homme du savoir de Balla! Après quelques instants de silence, Bakary exerça toute sa verve pour exagérer les derniers exploits (entendez les dernières roueries) du vieux sorcier défunt. (**180**)

Indeed, such intolerance seems incompatible with the prudent bet-hedging of 'Mais on était Malinké, et le Malinké ne reste jamais sur une seule rive' (**132**), though the parenthetical jibe, hardly one of the *de mortuis* variety, is to a degree purged of its shabbiness by the narrator's authority. But perhaps he is not atypical of his people in displaying extremes of prejudice, for elsewhere, when their religious relativism and canny native pragmatism are discussed, we read:

> Sont-ce des féticheurs? Sont-ce des musulmans? Le musulman écoute le Koran, le féticheur suit le Koma; mais à Togobala, aux yeux de tout le monde, tout le monde se dit et respire musulman, seul chacun craint le fétiche. Ni margouillat ni hirondelle! (**105**).

Perhaps here one might say that the propagandist momentarily gives way to the 'frère de plaisanterie'. Among the mourners who demand the kind of handouts that Fama is more used to receiving are his 'brethren in joke' (**127**; in current parlance, 'joke brother' is idiomatically suspect), linked in a non-aggression pact with the Doumbouya family that does not preclude a little ritual joshing. Elsewhere, King Djigui is saved from the wrath of the French colonial forces by the refusal of his interpreter, a 'brother' of this kind, to translate an intemperate reply (*Monnè*, p. 37).

When, on his release from imprisonment, Fama gives the cold shoulder to Bakary, the griot-narrator self-righteously notes: 'Les causeries entre la panthère et l'hyène honorent la seconde mais rabaissent la première' (**183**). But on the page facing (in the reference edition at least) stood the sound advice to warm himself by the new suns, i.e. move with the times, and eat what's on his plate:

> ... tu n'es pas un serval qui préfère mourir de faim plutôt que de se repaître de la viande qu'on lui a servie, quand cette viande n'est pas celle d'un animal qu'il a chassé. (**182**)

Bakary is objectively correct, and one recalls Count Mosca's aphorism: 'De tout temps les vils Sancho Pança l'emporteront à longue sur les sublimes don Quichotte' (Stendhal, *La Chartreuse de Parme*, I, 10). So though not helpful to Fama, such a juxtaposition is a valuable interpretative tool for the reader. Alternatively put, the presence in any text of the implied author,[17] judging in accordance with less self-interested and more elevated norms, could hardly be sensed more deeply than here. For all its ubiquity in *Les Soleils des Indépendances*, the griot's 'spin' is not intended ultimately to prevail.

---

[17] On the implied author, see, for instance, Shlomith Rimmon-Kenan, *Narrative Fiction: Contemporary Poetics* (London and New York: Methuen, 1988 [1983]), pp. 86-89 [p. 87]: '... while the narrator can only be defined circularly as the narrative 'voice' or 'speaker' of a text, the implied author is—in opposition and by definition—voiceless and silent.'

Conclusion

> *[T]he impotence of its selfish, angry present of masks and parodies, stifled and twisted by the insupportable, unrejected burden of its past, staring into the bleakness of its impoverished future.*

If the above quotation from Salman Rushdie[1] may be nudged slightly away from its focus on the alienation of the metropolis—which in any case is a large part of Fama's problem—it seems emblematic of *Les Soleils des Indépendances*, in which the protagonist can neither abide the present, escape the past, nor envisage the future. Profoundly mistrustful of the 'national discourse of the teleology of progress', he is somewhat too addicted to past glories in which 'the "timeless" discourse of irrationality' (Bhabha, pp. 302; 294) is given free play. There is a polarity between these that requires sensitive mediation.

Much critical toner has been spilt over Fama's tragic destiny. Epic grandeur and significance are conferred on his death, and if not much of the novel is 'told in a formal and elevated style',[2] then this part is: the birds of the air and the beasts of the field 'les premiers comprirent la portée historique du cri de l'homme', which resonates through 'tout le Horodougou', even as far-flung as the last prince of his line imagines it to be (**192**).[3] However, as stated above (p. 38), any consideration of 'tragic' in the Racinian sense of the term, derived from Aristotle's writings, that would involve *anagnorisis* (recognition) of the reasons for one's fate is more appropriate to Salimata, on whose dazed internal monologue the first part ends (**78**).

The contrast between the burlesque and the tragic lies in the juxtaposition of Fama's kingly disposition—enhanced by the attentions of his griot and his traditional healer, who address him as 'maître'—and the paucity of his inheritance. The protagonist is by

---

[1] *The Satanic Verses* (Dover, DE: The Consortium Inc., 1988), p. 320, (mis)quoted in Bhabha, p. 319.

[2] Abrams, p. 53.

[3] A similar exodus of all the inhabitants of the dictator's game reserve is provoked by the false rumour of the death of Koyaga (*En attendant*, pp. 376-80).

turns petulant—'Maussade! C'est un Fama maussade: cils aigres, cils rocailleux, lèvres tirées' **(114)**—and regal: 'Fama, coléreux, d'un mouvement de la main droite éteignit net. Balla ne sera pas de l'escorte' (*ibid.*). Any roseate view of his responsibilities as chief quickly disappears when he finds the dunghill on which he must be cockerel, and there is humour in the process of disabusal begun by Diakité **(83)** and his return to a homeland 'qui fut démembré et appartenait désormais à deux républiques' **(99)**. Which makes Fama rather the actor in a tragedy of the Shakespearean variety, in which both tragic and humorous situations can coexist, or a tragicomedy, taken in the most general sense of the term (i.e. without there being a happy end), or even the cross between epic and tragedy known as heroic tragedy.[4] If these labels seem still too grand to fit, then a definition from Chaucer that is baggier still seems to chime in with Fama's self-pitying inquisitorial arithmomania ('occupé à dénombrer les bâtardises des soleils des Indépendances'—**55**) and sterile feeling of exasperation **(11)**.[5] And if we were looking for examples of prophetic (or unconscious) irony tragically to be fulfilled in the text, then perhaps there is no need to look further than an apparently innocuous remark such as 'Mais on était Malinké, et un Malinké ne reste jamais sur une seule rive' **(132)**, a dilemma which only death will resolve for Fama.

The last chapter ended by comparing two animal behavioural maxims: the one about the fussy tiger-cat quoted to Fama by Bakary, and the griot's sententious narratorial intervention about the panther and the hyena. If a general moral to *Les Soleils des Indépendances* as cautionary tale were to emerge, as well as 'Move with the times' it could be along the lines of 'Beware of servile flatterers', examples of which are bound to be found in La Fontaine, and are.[6] Of course the flatterer here, though it would appear from his demeanour to be Bakary, turns out to be the griot, who encourages his master's

---

[4] Abrams, pp. 214-5.
[5] 'Tragedy is to seyn a certyn storie, / As olde bookes maken us memorie, / Of hym that stood in greet prosperitee, / And is yfallen out of heigh degree / Into myserie, and endeth wrecchedly' (*The Monk's Tale*).
[6] La Fontaine, *Fables*, I, 2: 'Le Corbeau et le Renard'; VIII, 14: 'Les Obsèques de la Lionne'.

fantasies of legitimacy and anachronistic modes of behaviour. But does Fama heed Bakary? No, he is in his own bubble by this time, not vocal in his dissent but just as dignified in his ominous silence. And before this, even the servile and self-interested advice of Diamourou and Balla, with the voiceover of the narrator ('Une vraie entreprise de possédé!'—**146**), had been rejected by Fama when he returned to the capital.

Les Soleils des Indépendances may be read as a parable which charts the hero's evolution from vain complainer, constantly deploring his lot and the lack of respect of his peer group ('Mânes de Moriba, fondateur de la dynastie! il était temps, vraiment temps de s'apitoyer sur le sort du dernier et légitime Doumbouya!' [**17**]), to true prince. The experience of prison changes Fama irrevocably and, once released, he focuses solely on his return to Togobala. He turns to a set of personal values which are superimposed on his Muslim and animist belief systems, providing another dimension to his character. The final dream of Fama, no doubt morphine-induced and deadening his hold on time chronology,[7] finds him regally seated on a white charger, like prestigious forebear Souleymane (**98**), like Djigui Keita on his white mare Sogbê (*Monnè*, p. 44), remembering back to his childhood and fulfilling his fantasy of power (**195-6**; see also **21**; **97-98**; **102**; **171**). Suddenly abandoned by his entourage, he panics and the horse judders to a halt on the edge of a precipice; then finally, coming to a place of peace, he attains, for the first time in the novel, a sense of comfort and contentment. This willingness to accept his destiny may be interpreted in terms of the evolution of the continent of Africa. Notwithstanding the ironic arm's length at which Allah and the ancestors are kept throughout the novel, the final chapters, during which the narrative conveys a sense of fulfilment of prophecy, propose that a spiritual life is a prerequisite for moral values. These will, in turn, change the future of Africa and Africans for the better. Kourouma's parable portrays the good and the bad of African traditional beliefs without sentimentality or

---

[7] See the unusual tense sequence of 'Deux infirmiers le maîtrisaient sur le brancard. Un autre agitait une seringue. A-t-il été piqué?' (**195**).

nostalgia, and traces a destiny for Africa which is related to authenticity and the pursuit of a spiritual life.

There is a paradox at the core of the reader's reaction to *Les Soleils des Indépendances*, in that the subject of the novel is the tragedy of a wasted life, representative of many thousands of lives across the African continent which have been destroyed by colonialism and by the post-independence era. This novel of visionary prescience is an attempt to call to account Côte d'Ivoire in particular, and Africa in general, for the post-independence excesses of corruption, megalomania, ideological tyranny and xenophobia in which they now fester. For reasons of no doubt justifiable caution, the president of the transparently fictionalised country is portrayed in a moment of clemency and generosity, but Kourouma's next novel will harshly castigate his fellow countrymen for having fallen for a hotchpotch of 'slogans qui à force d'être galvaudés nous ont rendus sceptiques, pelés, demi-sourds, demi-aveugles, aphones, bref plus nègres que nous ne l'étions avant et avec eux' (*Monné*, p. 278). In a piece of homophonic wordplay (italicised), the second of whose elements recalls the epic style of narration adopted by Kourouma, a pledge is made on which he will deliver in increasingly generous measure with each succeeding novel:

> Le sous-développement, la corruption, l'impudence avec laquelle sont employés les mots authenticité, socialisme, lutte et développement, cet ensemble de mensonges et de ressentiments, qui révoltent, ont des causes profondes et nombreuses. Le jour qu'il nous sera permis de dire et d'écrire autre chose que les louanges du parti unique et de son président fondateur, nous les *compterons* et les *conterons*. (*ibid.*, p. 276)

Tragedy predominates, 'le désespoir, l'«afro-pessimisme»' felt by spin doctor Maclédio (*En attendant*, p. 153) seems inéluctable, and yet the final words of the author that appear in print show a young lad waiting for the dawn of a new day, and the definite prospect of a minibus ride from a transport stand: 'Et il y avait des gbagas pour Bouaké' (*Quand on refuse*, p. 140). *Les Soleils des Indépendances*, as all of the novels, is full of depressing subject matter, yet a true tonic and a pleasure to read. Why is this so? The key to the paradox lies in the vitality of the language: Kourouma's style is irrepressible, innovative and revolutionary, reflecting the real patterns of speech and the culture and traditions of a people, as well as the essential humour and *joie de vivre* of the author. Unresentful (see *supra*, p. 59), he is at the same time unassimilated:

> Kourouma contamine le français classique par sa langue maternelle, le malinké, procédé qui lui permet d'exprimer son identité africaine dans un langage accessible à un grand public, et de régler ses comptes, à sa manière, avec le passé colonial de son pays. Ainsi, Kourouma joue un rôle de lien modéré entre les mondes africain et occidental, et son écriture s'accorde mal avec le parti pris anti-occidental pour lequel est censé opter la littérature postcoloniale.[8]

Like Proust and Joyce, he contributes originality and innovation to the novel form through the workings of style and the reinvention of language:

> Nous apporterons à la francophonie des techniques de conter et nous apporterons à la mondialisation la cosmogonie de nos peuples, la structure de nos langues qu'au fond nous avons créée et qui est la quintessence de notre génie. Et [elles] doivent entrer dans la mondialisation, pour que cette mondialisation soit le fruit de toutes les connaissances du monde: constituée par les différences de tous les peuples.[9]

---

[8] Emma Hartkamp, '*Les Soleils des Indépendances* d'Ahmadou Kourouma: de la théorie au roman', *Francophone Postcolonial Studies*, 2.1 (spring / summer 2004), 27-36 (p. 27).

[9] Ouédraogo, p. 779; edit in the original.

Glossary of terms

Page numbers denote the initial occurrence of a word or expression, which is glossed, since there are often other possibilities (e.g. Cafre, Dioula), according to its meaning in the context of the novel.

Affranchi (**110**)	freed slave.
alphatia (**117**)	opening *sourate* (q.v.) of Qur'an.
Balafon (**143**)	native musical instrument.
Bambara (**18**)	ethnicity of N.W. Côte d'Ivoire.
baobab (**33**)	baobab tree.
bissimilai (**72**)	priestly invocation of Allah's mercy, lit. 'In the name of the Lord'.
boubou (**13**)	long tunic of male Muslims.
broussard (**177**)	up-country hick.
bubale (**73**)	antelope.
Cabrin (**17**)	goat.
caféier (**161**)	coffee shrub / bush.
Cafre (**105**)	pagan, animist.
caïman (**163**)	cayman crocodile, giant alligator.
calao (**134**)	hornbill.
calebasse (**9**)	gourd.
canari (**102**)	earthenware pot.
cancrelat (**137**)	cockroach.
cauri (**68**)	cowrie shell (used to summon spirits).
cha-cha (**46**)	maraca-type percussion drum.
chéchia (**134**)	fez.
chefferie (**113**)	chief's jurisdiction.
chevrotain (**126**)	musk-deer.
cola (**16**)	cola / kola nut (a prestigious gift).
concession (**53**)	family compound.
cordier (**143**)	rope-maker.
Côte des Ébènes (**86**)	= Côte d'Ivoire.
cynocéphale (**18**)	dog-faced baboon.

Démarabouter (se) (**163**)	clear up / get straightened out.
Dioula (**13**)	Malinké merchant class
dja (**113**)	spirit / *Doppelgänger*.
dolo (**98**)	beer brewed from millet.
Échassier (**60**)	wader.
El Hadji (**140**)	who has made a pilgrimage to Mecca.
éléphantiasis (**160**)	elephantiasis.
excision (**33**)	clitoridectomy/female genital cutting.
Fama (**11**)	lit. 'rich and influential person'.
fétiche (**38**)	fetish mask or other object.
féticheur (**38**)	witch-doctor, medicine man.
flamboyant (**94**)	flame tree.
fonio (**113**)	cereal (eleusine or African millet), made into semolina or beer.
Foula (**161**)	of the Peul ethnicity.
fourmi magna (**15**)	flesh-eating ant.
foutou (**140**)	yam and banana, or plantain, dish.
francolin (**158**)	wild fowl.
francs (quinze) (**59**)	of Communauté financière d'Afrique (francs CFA); = c. 2p, then and now.
frère de plaisanterie (**127**)	brother in joke; non-aggression pact, but not excluding ritualised 'sledging'.
fromager (**22**)	silk-cotton tree.
Garde-cercle (**23**)	local policeman.
gnamakodé (**11**)	bastardy (from *gnama*, evil spirit).
goyave (**20**)	guava.
grateron (**168**)	woodruff.
gri-gri (**29**)	amulet, charm, magic potion.
griot (**11**)	propagandist, authoritative spin doctor of a noble family's history.
Harmattan (**21**)	Hot, dry wind blowing from east in November.
Horodougou (**21**)	Worodougou, 'lit. 'land of free men.'
houmba! (**110**)	expression of gratitude, thanks.

Glossary

Igname (**108**)   yam.
Indépendances (**9**)   from Dec. 1958 in Côte d'Ivoire.

Jujubier (**66**)   jujube tree.

Kala (**125**)   evil genius.
kapok (**104**)   from the *kapokier* (kapok tree).
karité (arbre de) (**94**)   karite or shea tree (*beurre de karité* is moisturising galam or shea butter).
Keita (**13**)   ethnicity chronicled in *Monnè*; (griot's mistake is hardly humiliating).
Koma (**105**)   freemasonry of *féticheurs*.

Lagune (**11**)   locates 'la capitale' on coast, i.e. it is Abidjan.
latérite (**12**)   red or brown rock.
léporide (**168**)   leporide (hare).
lougan (**97**)   cultivated family plot.

Malinké, malinké (**9**)   Of the Malinké ethnicity.
mânes (**17**)   shades, ancestral spirits.
mangouste (**62**)   mongoose.
manguier (**121**)   mango tree.
marabout (**21**)   Muslim holy man, soothsayer.
maraboutage (**23**)   jiggery-pokery, skullduggery.
marabouter (**23**)   to plot.
margouillat (**38**)   grey lizard.
marigot (**24**)   stream (often just a dry bed).

N'goni, n'goumé (**143**)   traditional dances.
ni (**113**)   soul.
Nikinai (**83**)   = Guinea.

Oryctérope (**85**)   aardvark.
Oulof (**64**)   ethnicity based in Senegal.
Ouassoulou (**13**)   region of S.W. Mali.
ourebi (**98**)   time of third Muslim prayer (16H30).

Pagne (**33**)   wraparound skirt.
paillote (**64**)   straw hut.

palabre (**14**) — palaver, (prolonged) discussion.
pangolin (**20-21**) — scaly anteater.
patate douce (**161**) — balmy (of weather).
Peul (**85**) — ethnicity of northern Côte d'Ivoire & Fouta Djallon massif of S. Guinea.
piler (**55**) — pound with long-handled pestle.
pilot (**18**) — pile, pillar (= *pilotis*).
pluvian (**161**) — wader.

Rémige (**108**) — wing feather.
République des Ébènes (**156**) — Côte d'Ivoire.

Samory (**18**) — Samory Touré, warrior leader.
  samoriennes, guerres (**112**) — his resistance in the Manding lands, pacified by French in the 1890s.

sel gemme (**26**) — rock salt.
serval (**182**) — serval.
silure (**103**) — silurid fish.
sirocco (**104**) — hot, scorching wind from Sahara.
sorgho (**187**) — sorghum.
sourate (**29**) — 'book' or 'chapter' of the Qur'an.

Talibet (**97**) — student of the Qur'an.
tisserin (**40**) — weaver bird.
tô (**95**) — sort of maize polenta.
toto (**129**) — louse ('monkey' more likely?).
Togobala (**98**) — lit. 'large village of straw huts' (two terms conflated in this first mention).

Toubab (**14**) — white man.
trigle (**167**) — tiny insect.
  ne pas casser la tête du petit trigle sans les yeux — not to do things by halves, get to the bottom of something.

Vanneau (**161**) — lapwing / peewit / plover.
varan (**103**) — lizard.
ver de Guinée (**169**) — guinea worm.
vituler (se) (**155**) — flop down and writhe about.

Yagba (**143**) — Malinké dance.

Select bibliography

Works by Ahmadou Kourouma

Novels

Les Soleils des Indépendances. Paris: Seuil, 1970.
Paperback, Seuil, coll. 'Points', P166.

Monnè, outrages et défis. Paris: Seuil, 1990.
Paperback, Seuil, coll. 'Points', P556.

En attendant le vote des bêtes sauvages. Paris: Seuil, 1998.
Paperback, Seuil, coll. 'Points', P762.

Allah n'est pas obligé. Paris: Seuil, 2000.
Paperback, Seuil, coll. 'Points', P940.

Quand on refuse on dit non, ed. G. Charpentier. Paris: Seuil, 2004.
Paperback, Seuil, coll. 'Points', P1377.

Theatre

Le Diseur de vérité. Châtenay-Malabry: Éditions Acoria, 1998.

Children's literature

Yacouba, le chasseur africain. Paris: Gallimard Jeunesse, 1998.

Le Chasseur, héros africain. Paris: Gallimard Jeunesse, 1999.

Le Griot, homme de paroles. Orange: Grandir, 1999.

Interviews with Ahmadou Kourouma, etc.

Badday, Moncef S., 'Ahmadou Kourouma, écrivain africain', *L'Afrique littéraire et artistique*, 10 (1970), 2-8.

Chemain, A., 'Ahmadou Kourouma, Le 20e anniversaire des *Soleils*', 'Littérature et francophonie', numéro special de *Écrire de l'école à l'université*, (Nice: C.R.D.P., 1989), 89-92.

Chemla, Y., '*En attendant le vote des bêtes sauvages*, ou le donsomana: entretien avec Ahmadou Kourouma', *Notre Librairie: Revue des Littératures du Sud*, 136 (janvier-avril 1999), 26-29.

Corcoran, P., 'Ahmadou Kourouma, 1927-2003', *Francophone Postcolonial Studies*, 2.1 (spring / summer 2004), 87-98.

Kourouma, A., *Je témoigne pour l'Afrique*. Grigny: Paroles d'aube, 1998.

Ouédraogo, J., 'Entretien avec Ahmadou Kourouma', *French Review*, LXXIV, 4 (March 2001), 772-85.

Critical studies of *Les Soleils des Indépendances*

Books

Borgomano, M., *Ahmadou Kourouma, le «guerrier» griot*. Paris: L'Harmattan, 1998.

Gassama, M., *La Langue d'Ahmadou Kourouma ou le français sous le soleil d'Afrique*. Paris: Éditions Karthala; A.C.C.T., 1995.

Jeusse, M.-P., '*Les Soleils des Indépendances*'. *Étude critique*. Paris: Nathan; Abidjan: Nouvelles Éditions Africaines, 1984.

M'lanhoro, M., *Essai sur 'Les Soleils des Indépendances' (Ahmadou Kourouma)*. Abidjan: Nouvelles Éditions Africaines, 1977.

Nicolas, J.-C., *Comprendre 'Les Soleils des Indépendances'*. Issy-les-Moulineaux: Les Classiques africains, 1985.

Nkashama, P.N., *Kourouma et le mythe: une lecture de 'Les Soleils des Indépendances'*. Paris: Éditions Silex, 1985.

Articles, chapters in books, etc.

Aire, V.-O., 'Fléau ou bénédiction: problématique de la ville dans trois romans ouest-africains', *Nouvelles du Sud*, 8 (1987), 75-85.

Bhabha, H.K., 'DissemiNation: Time, Narrative, and the Margins of the Modern Nation', in *Nation and Narration*, ed. H.K. Bhabha (London and New York: Routledge, 1990), pp. 291-322.

Britwum, K., 'Tradition and Social Criticism in Ahmadou Kourouma's *Les Soleils des Indépendances*', in K. Ogungbesan (ed.), *New West African Literature* (London: Heinemann, 1979), pp. 80-90.

Brunzin, M., 'Il Sincretismo linguistico nei romanzi di Ahmadou Kourouma', *Annali di Ca' Foscari: Revista della Facoltà e Letterature Straniere dell'Università di Venezia*, XXXVI, 1, 2 (1997), 279-98.

Chevrier, J., '*Les Soleils des Indépendances* d'Ahmadou Kourouma: une écriture nouvelle', *Notre Librairie*, 60 (juin-août 1981), 70-75.

Colvin, M., 'La Profanation du sacré: l'inscription du tragique dans deux romans d'Ahmadou Kourouma', *Études Francophones*, XV, 2 (automne 2000), 37-48.

Derive, J., 'L'Utilisation de la parole orale traditionnelle dans *Les Soleils des Indépendances* d'Ahmadou Kourouma', *L'Afrique littéraire*, 54-55 (1979-1980), 103-10.

Echenim, K., 'La Structure narrative des *Soleils des Indépendances* d'A. Kourouma', *Présence Africaine*, 107 (3e trimestre, 1978), 139-61.

Emeto-Agbasière, J., 'Le Proverbe dans le roman africain', *Présence Francophone*, 29 (1986), 27-41.

Gourdeau, J.-P., 'L'Islam dans *Les Soleils des Indépendances*', *Nouvelles du Sud*, 6-7 (1986-1987), 139-42.

Huannou, A., 'La Technique du récit et le style dans *Les Soleils des Indépendances*', *L'Afrique Littéraire et Artistique*, 38 (1975), 31-38.

Ireland, K.R., 'End of the Line: Time in Kourouma's *Les Soleils des Indépendances*', *Présence Francophone*, 23 (automne 1981), 79-89.

Kern, A., 'On *Les Soleils des Indépendances* and *Le Devoir de violence*', *Présence Africaine*, 85 (1973), 209-30.

Koné, A., 'L'Effet de réel dans les romans de Kourouma', *Études françaises*, XXXI, 1 (été 1995), 13-22.

Langlois, É., '*Les Soleils des Indépendances*, roman de la stérilité', *Présence Francophone*, 8 (printemps 1974), 95-102.

Lavergne, É., '*Les Soleils des Indépendances* et l'authenticité romanesque', *Éthiopiques*, 39 (n.s. II, 4) (1984), 72-84.

Michaud, G., 'Représentations culturelles dans *Les Soleils des Indépendances* d'Ahmadou Kourouma', *Ethnopsychologie*, XXXV, 2-3 (avril-septembre 1980), 136-44.

Mortimer, M., 'Prince of a Vanishing Kingdom: Ahmadou Kourouma', in *Journeys through the French African Novel* (Portsmouth, NH: Heinemann; London: James Currie, 1990), pp. 106-119.

Ohaegbu, A. U., '*Les Soleils des Indépendances* ou le drame de l'homme écrasé par le destin', *Présence Africaine*, 90 (1974), 53-60.

Ouattara, A., 'Analyse linguistique des temps verbaux dans un extrait de *Les Soleils des Indépendances* d'A. Kourouma', *Langage et l'Homme: Recherches Pluridisciplinaires sur le Langage*, XXXV, 2-3 (septembre 2000), 139-51.

Schikora, R.G., 'Narrative Voice in Kourouma's *Les Soleils des Indépendances*', *French Review*, LV, 6 (May 1982), 811-7.

Soubias, P., 'Deux langues pour un texte: problèmes de style chez Ahmadou Kourouma', *Champs du Signe: Sémantique, Poétique, Rhétorique*, 5 (1995), 209-22.

Toyo, A., 'Carnavalisation et dialogisme dans *Les Soleils des Indépendances* d'Ahmadou Kourouma', *Francofonia: Studi e Ricerche sulle Letterature di Lingua Francese*, XVI, 30 (primavera 1996), 99-111.

Uwah, G.O., 'Waiting and Disenchantment: Kourouma's *Les Soleils des Indépendances* and Oupoh's *En attendant la liberté*', *Afrika Focus*, III, 1-2 (1987), 65-80.